G R JORDAN

The Fairy Pools Gathering

A Patrick Smythe Mystery Thriller

Contents

Foreword

This story is set on the Isle of Skye. Although set amongst known towns and landmarks, note that all persons and specific places are fictional and not to be confused with actual buildings and structures that exist and which have been used as an inspirational canvas on which to tell a completely fictional story.

Acknowledgement

To Susan, Harold, Evelyn, Pete, Joan, Jean and Rosemary for your work in bringing this novel to completion, your time and effort is deeply appreciated.

Practiced poorly, tourism can be extremely negative.

Edward Norton

Chapter One

Today is hot and sunny, and I mean, as we say in Ulster, proper sunshine, not the occasional bit you get here and there. This is real August weather. The sun is blazing and I'm in my short sleeves, standing at the back of the sixteenth green. The Royal Cairn's Golf Club has never looked so good. Well, actually it has. You see, with the sun comes a little bit of burning of the greens, and some of them are more browns than greens. But in fairness, they still putt well and they're still holding their own. I'm watching my work partner, and coincidentally golf partner, lining up a putt. It's thirty feet away but she's staring at a birdie. This is significant because over the last seven holes, she's single handedly taken us from the position of being two holes down to now being two up, and with this putt to win the hole, we can win the match. That will get me out of the sunshine into the shade for a nice cup of tea.

My partner's name is Susan Calderwood and she works for me as my assistant in my private investigation business. It's a cosy arrangement as I'm currently dating her mother as well. I first came across Susan in an investigation into members of this Golf Club. She's a bit of a star on the greens and I'm calmly leaning with my single arm on my putter. There's something kind of wrong when we play golf as our opponents invariably watch me, fascinated by how a one-armed man can actually play golf but the real star is Susan. They don't bother giving her a handicap anymore, or maybe they do. Maybe it's me.

The red ponytail falls down the side of her neck as she leans over her putt, staring intently at the white ball before her feet. The putter goes back, gently swings forward, strikes the ball, which starts off to the right, then swings back across the hill then back right, following the contours of the green. Her face says it's going to come up short but it's not. She gets tentative and I'm left alone believing about her putt. Everything's just not quite right and yet it always is. Like those people that go into exams, claiming how worried they are, how nervous, and come out with a one-hundred percent. The ball hasn't dropped and I'm walking over to our opponents ready to shake hands. It's time for a cup of tea.

The club balcony is the venue for this cup of tea and our opponents buy the round which must be one of the cheapest they've ever had as Susan's having a fizzy drink and I'm having a cup of tea. I can go a couple of gin and tonics but I rarely drink during the day. The conversation's flowing with this husband and wife team although in honesty, it's really them talking about themselves. I nod along politely, Susan too, but when the phone goes, I instantly jump up, saying I must take this call.

It's a woman on the line, calling herself Ingrid Appleton. She says she lives in Kyle and she has some issues she needs to discuss with me. I ask what and she says she doesn't want to say over a phone but it concerns her immediate family and she'd like to meet as soon as possible. I've just played a round of golf and I'm tired, so I tell her that I can't meet her until tomorrow and she's welcome to come down into the office in Stranraer. That would be a long drive for anyone and when she suggests a compromise of Oban, I accept. Returning to the balcony, I drink the rest of my tea quickly and make my excuses with Susan to leave our golfing partners. I am a loner though I don't mind good conversation. But when other people just talk about themselves, I tend to bow out pretty quickly, especially when they keep going on about how good their golfing is . . . having just been kicked by us.

Susan's a bit annoyed at me today because I've decided to take the drive up to Oban on my own. This is to make sure that I get some clear time from her because as keen as she is, which is nice, she's been peppering me with questions about the last few cases we've done, pointing out how she would play it; how she would do this, how she would do that, and begging for a chance to do some more work on her own. Last time we had a serious case in Mull, I had to let her go on her own at times and I wasn't quite sure if she was ready for it. But circumstances forced my hand and now she wants to operate on her own all the time. Don't get me wrong; she's capable but sometimes she hasn't seen enough to know what she's getting into.

Praise the Lord for air-conditioned cars. Today's another hot one with hardly a cloud in the sky, that incessant blue taking over, except for the one bit of sky you can't look at because the sun's beating down so hard at you. The venue for the meeting is a rather drab drive-by, a remnant of the past. In days gone by, they'd have called it a greasy spoon—now it's just a traditional cafe.

The exterior is white and drab, the wooden-framed windows needing some paint. In fact, the whole building needs a complete makeover and I think I should apply on its behalf to one of those programs on TV. Maybe they could change it in forty-eight hours; they certainly couldn't make it any worse.

I'm dressed in a dark blue jacket, casual, with jeans, trying to look reasonably smart for a new client but as I walk in, I think I shouldn't have bothered. It's three in the afternoon and there's only four clients in this cafe, of which three are eating. One looks like a delivery driver and he still has his jacket with logo on. Another is a young kid, with a mother who looks too young, eating chips with ketchup splashed all over and then there's a woman who I presume to be Ingrid Appleton. This is because she's raising her hand and waving it at me. I guess I'm easy to spot with a missing arm.

I slide myself into the seat opposite and see a slightly overweight woman who's dressed for the sun. She's wearing a white top, one of those with the thin strap and it hugs her body but not in an alluring way, but rather picks up the rolls of fat that exist around her. She can only be in her late twenties but her hair looks like it hasn't been washed in the last three days. She's wearing no makeup which is not a bad thing as I despise too much being used—maybe that's because I don't use it myself. Although you might not find that surprising as there's a lot of men who use a bit of touch up these days.

I notice the woman is wearing a pair of shorts and flip flops before I sit down and as she sits forward, I realize that the top is designed to show some cleavage. In all honesty, she doesn't look a great sight. I hope I'm not being sexist saying that but because I don't look a great sight myself, I feel I can comment. Yes, I try to keep in shape; there's not a lot of fat on me but not so that I have one of those bodies that people look at and swoon. Rather, I have one of those that annoy people because it doesn't carry a lot of weight despite the amount I eat but neither does it give that muscle man view. I'm more sinew than muscle—or light on my feet as I prefer to say.

'Mrs Appleton, I presume.'

'Hello, Mr Smythe, thank you for coming. I need you to investigate my husband.'

Here we go again. More than half of the cases I take on are because of infidelity, husbands running around, wives on the sly, people finding someone else to keep them entertained. There's a lot of it going on, and for private investigators, it tends to be our bag because a lot of the time, the law hasn't been broken so the police aren't interested. We're also discreet, just in case the client happens to be wrong.

There's a misconception that goes around about private investigators. People think these stunningly beautiful men and women come to see us and tell us about affairs that are happening. Then it turns out to be multiple people involved, all completely stunning and gorgeous and somehow the business we're employed in—that is, to take photographs and prove what's happening—is somehow like a movie where we can enjoy all the figures involved. This is not so; quite often some of the sights you see might make you want to vomit rather than desire to take part.

'Tell me your story, Mrs Appleton, starting with your name, where you live, and what's the problem.'

'Mr Smythe, my name is Ingrid Appleton and I live in Kyle, the block house just by the bridge there. We've lived up there for a couple of years now and my husband—he works in the tourist sector in Skye—has to travel across the bridge for meetings every week. His work has to do with accommodation and we have acquired a number of sites and usually we book up. He takes care of that side of the business, not me, you see.

I'm sitting at home with a couple of children to bring up. I know you're looking at me and thinking she could do better, she could sort herself out but after a couple of kids, it's not easy, Mr Smythe, and I think it's turned him off, too. We used to have a good life, a good life in the bedroom but now there's nothing, I'm not sure how interested he is in me at all. I'm not yet thirty, Mr Smythe, and we should still be active. That's what they say, isn't it? That's the polite term?'

I nod and part of me rolls my eyes. *Here we go again.*

'You say he disappears during the week to meetings. What makes you think he's actually having an affair?'

'He's coming back late, extremely late, sometimes three in the morning. I ask him what that's about and he tells me he's tired, that the meetings went on. His meetings never went on like that; he was always back to the house by ten and that was irregularly then. It used to be normal days, but now he disappears for meetings at seven, eight, nine o'clock at night. Something is up, Mr Smythe, and I want you to find out. He's also got a lot more agitated.'

'How's the business doing, Mrs Appleton? Is he making good money?'

'We're making more money than ever, according to my bank balance,' she says. 'I don't take to do with the business but we seem to be doing very well. But in the past, when he did well, he would have bought me something or taken me out to dinner. He's just not engaged at all.'

'And what's his name?' I ask. 'And what does he look like?'

'His name is Alex and frankly I did well for myself. He was a rugby player and he stands six foot two, built like the proverbial brick house, although he's lost all his hair now. Not that that makes a difference these days—so many bald men on the telly

6

looking good, others shaving their hair to look like them. We met when I was at college and I fell for him quickly. I was there for three years and we moved in together afterwards, got married, had kids, moved to Skye, or rather to Kyle. We wanted to live on Skye, but we couldn't find a house so we ended up in Kyle instead. He bought businesses for the tourist industry in Skye; everything went fine and recently business has gone really well but he's just changed.

'This is going to sound personal,' I say, 'and forgive me if it sounds offensive, but you said that you lost your shape from having kids. Is that bothering him? Has he just gone off sex with you?' It's a bit of a harsh question and I can see the woman getting a little bit angry at me asking it but it's a particularly good point. She wants me to know what his behaviour is and she's assumed it's another woman. Sometimes, us men, and indeed, occasionally women, just strike out on different directions which have got nothing to do with our partners and more to deal with boredom in life. Maybe the tourism industry isn't what he wants it to be.

'Mr Smythe, last night, he came into the bedroom and I was getting changed. Not a look at me, not even a cheeky glance as I was standing in the altogether. In days gone by, I'd have felt hands on me, we'd have gone for a cheeky fumble at least if not gone at it right there on the bed. He's having an affair, trust me.'

I continue the conversation but in truth, there's little else to pick up. She gives me her address, the addresses of some of the accommodations he looks after on Skye and it feels like a fairly run-of-the-mill investigation. I drive back down in the afternoon sun and make my way back to Maggie's house where I'm staying and find her in the back garden sunning herself. I haven't seen a bikini on her often and that's because she's got that worry a lot of women have about their shape after kids. Her kids are long gone but she still thinks she hasn't settled back to the way she was before. In truth, she probably hasn't. Not that I saw back then but she puts too much stake on this. I think she still looks great and the odd wrinkle and that, it doesn't do any harm at all.

'I'll take a beer,' she says, hearing me arrive, 'and then you can sit and enjoy the view. It's not often I wear this.' I make myself a pot of tea, bring it with Maggie's beer, and sit with my shirt off. I think I last about an hour before I complain the sun's too hot and move into the shade. She stays there for another hour until she can hear Susan coming in.

'Anything new at work?' I ask her and she shakes her head. 'But I'm gonna catch some of these rays' she says, 'while the sun's like this.' She heads off upstairs and soon is back down in the garden lying beside her mother. Susan's nearly twenty and she's the daughter of a woman I'm falling very deeply for. Unfortunately, she's also got that ability to attract me as well and so when she lies in her bikini in the garden, I get up and tell Maggie I'm going for a walk. I guess Maggie understands because she says she's going to join me. Twenty minutes later, we're stopped off at the edge of a forest trail. I decided to go here because at least I can get some shade from the sun as I walk. Maggie's got a shirt on and her jeans and as we stroll along, she can read my face.

'What's up?'

'I think I'm going to send Susan away on her own, do a bit of work. I think she's ready for this one.'

'Oh,' she says, 'something interesting?'

I shake my head. 'Exactly the opposite, that's why I'm sending her; a husband cheating allegedly.'

'Well, you know your business,' she says. 'I'm happy it means that my sunbathing won't get disturbed by my daughter coming in and usurping me.'

'Sorry,' I say, 'it doesn't do me a lot of good with the pair of you side by side like that.'

She kisses me on the cheek. 'I know,' she says. 'At least, you have the wit to walk away.'

'Don't worry,' I say, 'there's nothing like the original.'

She punches me in the arm. 'You are one cheesy idiot.'

Chapter Two

With Susan away from the house, Maggie and myself try to take advantage and be a little bit more intimate. The problem is that Maggie's got another daughter, Kirsten, Susan's older sister, and she's still living here too. She's out most days working nine to five but with the sunshine, she's taken a few days off and we find her lingering around the house. I wake up one morning and I see Maggie at the window. She's standing in just a shirt and I take that as a cue that she must be cold and need a cuddle. This is a complete lie but it works for me and with my arm around her it appears to work for her. 'Let's go on your boat,' she says; 'let's get on Craigantlet and let's head off.'

'But that means the office will be unmanned, you know. I can't go too far,' I say.

'Stuff the office,' she says. 'The sun's up. We're going to get two weeks of this and I want to spend some time with you. Let's get on that boat, away from everything, and maybe you can see that bikini you like,' she says. I wrap my arm tightly around her indicating that would be nice but this apparently isn't enough for her. 'You can see me without the bikini if you want,' she says, 'but it's gonna be somewhere very, very out of the way.'

I laugh. 'I don't think it's the clothing that's holding me back,' I say; 'just business isn't exactly flying along at the moment.'

'But that will come, Paddy. Sort it—take three weeks off. If Susan wraps her case up, she'll be back; she can inform you about anything else but take three weeks with me. I'm here right now, ready, and I phoned up—I can get the time off at the hospital. I had to pull a few favours but you know what, I want time on board that boat with you on your own.'

When a woman talks to you like that, you don't say no. And so that day, I go to the office, shut it up, set up all my automatic answering machines and emails, and direct them to an account. I phone Susan, tell her what's happening, and tell her I don't want to hear from her unless she's having trouble.

She says she's following the man but so far there's nothing she can find out. It's been three days and so far, all he's done is check his businesses. He's gone outside, late at night once and that was just to do a spot of fishing. She's found nothing untoward about what he's doing.

'And this is what it's like,' I say to her over the phone. 'Ninety percent of what we do is boredom, keeping an eye on people doing nothing wrong. Just make sure you don't eat too many donuts while you do it.' I hear a laugh on the other end.

'You enjoy time away, you and Mum, and don't worry about this, Paddy, I can handle it,' she says. And that's the problem, she sounds so confident it makes me worried because I never feel like I can handle it. I always feel like somebody's going to trip me up.

The next two days on Craigantlet are some of the best I've had. I won't go into a lot of detail because frankly, that's private and you should be ashamed of yourself if you want to know details. What are you, some sort of Private Investigator? Let's

11

just say, Maggie and I had an exceptionally good time. We also did a lot of sailing though and we head up past Mull round towards Ardnamurchan point, heading up towards Mallaig. It's great being out on the water because it's cool and I can't sit in the sun for long. Maggie, in reality, is quite the same. She's got pale skin and she's never going to brown but being up on deck and jumping in to enjoy the water every now and again is quite something and this being Scotland, the water's certainly refreshing if not outright freezing.

We're sitting on deck enjoying a cup of tea and Maggie's got a bottle of wine open when the phone rings. It's a satellite phone because I'm out of mobile signal elsewhere otherwise.

'Leave it,' says Maggie; 'you're on holiday, just leave it.'

Standing up, I walk past her, putting my hand on her shoulder.' If someone's using this SAT phone, it's for a reason,' I say. 'Sorry. Susan's out in the field. If she's in trouble, I need to know.' I get the nod of approval from Maggie which I wasn't waiting for; it's just nice to have. The mention of her daughter being in trouble probably swung it. I bring the phone back on deck as I answer it.

'Yeah, it's Paddy.'

'Paddy, Susan. I need a little bit of help.' There's a concern in her voice.

'Are you in trouble?' I ask, 'How much help and how fast?'

'No, no,' she says, 'nothing like that. I haven't been spotted, people haven't been watching me. I've been watching other people but I've just seen something weird last night.'

'How do you mean weird?' I say because I've seen a lot of weird things in my time but, not all of it illegal. It was the man in the nappy with his mistress that was the best one for me. Well, the funniest one—best is probably the wrong word.

'I was tailing Appleton and I thought he was heading out for another night's fishing but then I noticed there were no rods in the car. He headed off into the middle of Skye to a place called the Fairy Pools. I don't know if you know it but a lot of waterfalls, quite picturesque but this was like midnight. As I got there, I was aware that there were other people about. He reaches into the car and takes out this white gown. Then he walks up by one of the pools and I can see them, there's at least ten men there and a couple of women. Then this other woman arrives and she starts dancing in front of them passing close to each one, stopping by them.

'Does she pass anything to them?' I ask.

'No, well not as far as I can see, she only seems to talk to them but she dances for maybe half an hour going between each one. Some of them are holding sticks with marks on them, all a bit strange, like the start of a horror film. You half expect her to be lying on a slab and getting stabbed by the end of it but she doesn't, she just dances around.'

'And is she in one of these white gowns as well?'

'No,' says Susan, 'it's hard to describe. It's almost like she's got lots and lots of veils on. It's thin material, but there's so much of it, you don't see anything,' she says. 'I mean, she's well covered. It's more like she's trying to look like a pixie or some sort of fairy.'

'Did you tail him afterwards?'

'Of course, I did,' says Susan, sounding a bit peeved at me for having asked such a question. 'And he went home, just went home. It was weird, Paddy; there wasn't anything particularly sexual about it. I just didn't know what to make of it at all. I've taken some footage of it but it is from quite a distance. I'm going to keep on him and see if he goes back and see if I can get some closer footage.'

'Hold off on that, send me the footage through and I'll tell you what we're going to do. What was the ratio of men and women?'

'Like I said, I think there was ten men. I would say there was another three women in the circle and then that woman who was dancing; it's not even like she was provocatively dancing with them. I just don't get it.'

It takes a while for the footage to download but when it does, I sit on the deck of Craigantlet with Maggie on my lap, holding my tablet in front of me. Just because I'm working doesn't mean I can't enjoy myself at the same time. The footage plays on the tablet and I see what is a forty-something-year-old woman dancing around like a pixie. The men are of all different ages but all dressed in these white gowns along with three women—one young, two older. There's chanting going on as well—although I'm not quite sure what it's saying; it's possibly a foreign language.

I phone Martha, my resident expert researcher to see if she can translate some of the language. She knows I'm on the boat with Maggie and tells me to leave it with her and get back to enjoying myself but I'm struggling and I guess it's the investigator in me. You see Martha lives somewhere else and I can hand this over to her and she'll assess it and she'll tell me what language has been spoken. She'll tell me all about what symbolism this is and that is and I can just forward that on to Susan, to get on with it.

But this is weird and I like investigating weird; I don't like things not being known. It's also weird enough that I'm wondering what Susan could be getting herself into. That afternoon I stand at the back of the boat, fishing line in the water when Maggie comes up behind me. She wraps her arms around me, gives my chest a rub and then she pulls tighter.

'I really didn't want you to answer that phone.'

'Sorry,' I say, 'Susan could have been in trouble. She needed help.'

'No, not that. For a couple of days, I had you, attention undivided, just you and me; now part of you is not here,' she says. 'Part of you is over there trying to work out what's going on.'

There's no point denying it—it's who I am so I just nod my head. 'Sorry,' I say, 'I'll try and put it out of my mind'

She pulls close. 'No, you won't. Well maybe you'll try but it'll just chip away at you. Put the rod away; let's get the boat up to Skye. Where do you want to go in, Portree or into Kyle?'

'I'm sorry,' I said. 'If it helps, Susan will have a car. Can probably get the boat on the South Side, away from a lot of people, run the tender in, and she could pick me up. You can bring the tender back up when I'm done. We can stay pretty secluded.'

'Secluded sounds good,' says Maggie.

The sun continues to beam down but the wind's refreshing as the boat makes its way along. I let Maggie steer, standing beside her, and we spend a couple of hours talking, sharing little things of our past which is probably a very healthy thing to do because although we've shared a lot over the last couple of days, there hasn't been a lot of talking with it. As the evening starts to fall, the SAT phone goes off again and picking it up, I announce Paddy, expecting to hear Martha or Susan on the other end. Instead, there's a different voice.

'Hello. Hello, is that Mr Smythe?'

'Yes. This is Patrick Smythe, how can I help you, sir?'

The voice is shaking, real uneasiness as if he scared. 'It's my wife, Mr Smythe. I'm worried about her. I think she's been blackmailed.'

'What makes you think this, sir?' I ask.

'She's just been acting strange, going to places late at night. I've tried following her but she shakes me off; it's out of character. I think she might be being used.'

'When you say used, sir, do you mean physically, sexually, or some other way?'

'God, I don't know. I really don't know but something's up with her. I need someone to look at it; I need someone to find out now.'

'And whereabouts are you, sir?' I ask.

'We're on Skye,' he says. The hairs prick up on the back of my neck. It's not unusual to have two jobs in the same area and be totally unrelated, but something about this has just got my nose sniffing and looking for a scent.

'I think I need to hear more about this,' I say; 'we need to meet. Whereabouts can you get to safely on Skye?'

'I can join you in Portree,' he says. 'Can you get to Portree?'

'I'll be there tomorrow,' I say, 'in the morning. Do you know of a nice little cafe somewhere reasonably quiet?' He gives me the details and I say I'll meet him there at ten. Putting the satellite phone away, I go back and put an arm around Maggie. I tell her what's happening. She leans back and we enjoy a long kiss together. When we break off she says out loud, 'I just wanted to mark the end of our few days together with something I enjoy.'

'We're still going to be together,' I say.

'Not in the same way,' she says. 'If you need any help, Paddy, I don't mind helping out on this one.'

'Let's see what it is first,' I say. 'When I know what's going on, I'll see if you can tag along. Otherwise you're just going to have to be that wonderful woman I race back to.'

'And I guess the boat's going into Portree then,' she says, 'not feeling though like that's very secluded, if I'm honest.'

'No,' I say. I hope she can hear the disappointment in my voice. We need to sail through the night to make Portree for morning and Maggie sends me to bed around about ten o'clock because I'm working in the morning but it's a fitful sleep. In my dreams I see someone dancing. She's going around some water, men in white gowns watching her, and then there's a stone slab and Christopher Lee stabbing her with some large knife. I look back at the men in white and they're wearing goat's horns on their heads and in their hands, there are animal skulls.

I wake up with a start at about four in the morning and begin to laugh at my dream. I paddle out of my room and up to where Maggie is steering. I smack her gently on the backside and she lifts up out of the seat, lets me slide in behind her before sitting on my lap.

'Not able to sleep, tiger?' she says. 'I knew that brain would be taking over.'

'You can blame it on Christopher Lee,' I say, 'killing off virgins again.'

She gives me a strange look before she scans the water making sure that there's nothing ahead of us. Then she looks at me again and then a third time. 'Never tell me what you dream of,' she says.

'Even if you're in it?' I say.

'Especially if I'm in it.'

I bury my head in the folds of her black hair falling down

17

her neck. I never saw who the woman on the altar was; I must check next time. Bet it was Maggie though.

Chapter Three

It's an overcast day as the boat sails into Portree. We moor up Craigantlet and I take the tender across, leaving Maggie in the bunk. She sailed all night and in fairness, she's shattered, so I'll try and stay away from her at least until late this afternoon and give her a chance to sleep.

Portree is a funny place with winding streets, quaint in its own way but probably the biggest place on the Skye. In the summer, Skye floods with tourists and becomes incredibly busy for the size of it and its facilities. But in winter, I think it's quainter and better to visit for then you see the place as it really is and not as a tourist haven. On the other hand, with not so many people about, you wouldn't make money and people have got to live. So, go when you want, take your pick but trust me, I prefer it in winter.

It doesn't take me long to find the café and when I enter I find there's no one there yet. It's eight o'clock in the morning and I said we'd meet at nine. That's the thing about being on the boat—you can work out roughly when you want to arrive but it doesn't always work out exactly and with Maggie requiring sleep, I just decided to get off as quick as I could. I could ring Susan but depending what she's been up to last night I might be waking her up as well. Although I wouldn't feel so bad about that as she is a paid employee if she's on stakeout. But after a stakeout at night, that wouldn't be very fair. So instead, I just relax, order some scrambled eggs with toast and a pot of tea.

The cafe is one of those pretty ones that tourists like to enjoy—wooden tables that don't look like they came from a budget Swedish store but instead have a bit more class to them. There are quaint mats in the middle of the table and the chairs don't rock; certainly the table feels like it's fixed properly to the ground. My tea comes in a proper China cup and I pay proper prices although don't get me wrong, it's not the Savoy. Around the walls are old style maps and there is a rack showing local events. Not tatty pamphlets either. Instead they look crisp and neat as if they've been ordered within the year and not just been sitting there from previous tourist seasons. This all tells me a bit about my client. He won't be bottom-end, in fact, he'll quite enjoy this type of thing and probably goes out to this sort of coffee house every day. So, I reckon he's middle class if that still exists, a reasonable income which all make sense if he thinks he's being blackmailed, especially if it's for money. There's no point blackmailing somebody who at the end of the day hasn't got any cash.

It's nine o'clock and I'm on my third cup of tea when a man walks in. He's quite diminutive. I would say five feet four and he is wearing a shirt and tie with a suit over it. It's grey and not too ostentatious, the tie being a neat blue. Dark blue, of course, speaks of somebody professional but not a sales or a marketing person. Someone wearing a suit and tie because that's what he does, not trying to sell anything about himself.

As he steps in, he looks around because by now, the place has five or six customers. I did give him that subtle hint in finding me, I'm the one without another arm and I can see him staring so I raise that single arm and wave him over.

I don't know what he was expecting, or maybe I do; perhaps he was looking for another man in the suit and a nice tie but at the end of the day, he's hired an investigator. I don't get paid to look good; I get paid to produce results and if he can't see past the fact I'm not wearing a suit, frankly, stuff him, he needs me. I've already got a case on the go.

'Good morning, sir. Take a seat and won't you have some coffee, maybe a cup of tea?'

'No, no,' he says nervously, 'I won't.' He starts looking around. And I wonder if he thinks he's being followed. 'I don't normally do this,' he says. 'Do you think some people here could be listening?'

'Only as much as people always listen in a café. Do you think you were tailed today?'

'Tailed?' he said. 'Oh right. Do you think I was?'

'I don't honestly know, sir, because I didn't follow you in your car but you haven't been tailed into here. There's no one come in since you arrived; there's no one looking in from outside and I've been watching these people all along. Did you tell anybody about meeting me here?' He shakes his head. 'Well, I didn't tell anybody either so no, I don't think you've been tailed and I think you should have a cup of tea or coffee. It just looks a bit strange if you come into a coffee house and don't drink anything.'

'All right, okay then, coffee, a pot of coffee.'

I wave over the woman behind the counter. She's got a neat white apron tied around her but when I give my order, she spins on her heel and waves over to a man behind that counter who immediately starts to make coffee. She is giving me the feeling she runs the place and when she asked if we want something else, I feel obliged to have another round of toast. I'm not hungry—it's just she had that imposing disposition.

'I'm Paddy Smythe, sir, and I investigate things. I understand you think your wife's having a bit of trouble. So, all I want you to do is tell me exactly what you think's happening. I don't care if you think it sounds ludicrous or strange, just tell me how you see it and I'll tell you afterwards if it's ludicrous or strange.' The man nods his head, looking around him once again and then begins to talk, only to be interrupted by the woman returning with my toast and his coffee. Once she steps away, he looks around himself again before starting over.

'My name is Eddie, or rather it's Edward, Edward Carnegie, and I work in an architect's firm in Kyle of Lochalsh. But I'm not here about that; I'm here about Jenny—that's my wife.'

'Do you have a photograph of her,' I say and he looks at me slightly shocked before reaching inside his wallet and handing it over. The man before me, I would say is mid-thirties, possibly early forties, but the woman I'm looking at is about forty-seven to forty-eight. I tell this from the eyes and the hairstyle; there's nothing flamboyantly younger about her and she has that greying look of the older women but blimey, she's in rather good nick. There's long blonde hair flowing down past the shoulders. The photograph's a full length one and she's standing in a smart skirt and blouse smiling back at whoever was taking the photograph.

'Go on, sir, you were telling me.'

'Well,' he says looking around him again. 'Jenny's been a little bit erratic of late, disappearing out in the evening, sometimes not coming back until quite late. At first, I thought,' he stutters at this point, 'at first, I thought maybe she had someone else.'

'Well, from her looks, that's not an unreasonable assumption but is that her nature?' I ask. 'Is she someone who flirts a lot? Has she been known to run off before?'

The man shakes his head. 'Never, she's never run off and that's what bothered me. She's always been my Jenny, Jenny and Eddie, that's what we always said. Always together but she became more secretive and I had noticed our account. It's a small one we have that we both dip into; we each have our separate ones where the main money goes. But we pool what's left over into the other one and it's used for the fun things in life, but I started to notice that there's money disappearing from it each month.'

'And how long have you noticed? How long has it been going on for?'

'I only realized it a couple of weeks ago but it's been happening over the last year and she's been different over the last year. I tried to tell myself nothing was really wrong but now I've found this, I think I can't look away anymore. I need someone to look at it. It's not been easy either because she's not a stupid woman—she knows I'm up to something. That's why I wanted to meet you here, away from everything. I couldn't meet you in Kyle; there's too many people there who know us, who know me.'

'Okay, sir, give me a few details of where you live and that, where you work, where she works and we'll run from there.' I take a drink of tea while he tells me several addresses, which I make a note of. He seems bothered by that, that I'm writing things down and again he's constantly looking around him.

'The café's beginning to fill up and I guess that's because the tourists are starting to move in, people in for an early morning scone and a cuppa before they walk round to the next sight. This seems to bother my client more than myself. When I ask him the next question, he fails to hear me being somewhat distracted, so I ask it again. 'Where do you think she's going when she disappears off?'

'I don't know,' he says, 'but I know this—she goes out dressed in her best.'

'What do you mean?' I say. 'What's she wearing?'

'Oh, she goes out in a tracksuit normally, jogging bottoms, sweats, top, but she is not out running or doing anything like that.'

'But you said she was going in her best, sir?'

'Yes,' he says, 'best underwear.'

I sit back in my seat a little bit bemused. 'Without wanting to be indelicate,' I say, 'how do you know this? Do you just . . . do you pop up to make sure each time? Have you some way of checking before she is out the door?'

'No,' he says, 'it's afterwards. She has one of her drawers where she keeps her better stuff, ones for special occasions, nothing funny, simply good quality, quite sexy stuff and it's gone but she's also wearing jogging bottoms, sweatshirts. It doesn't make sense.'

It doesn't but I ask again. 'You have no idea where she's going? Have you ever tried to tail her?'

'No,' he said, 'I wouldn't be able; she'd spot me a mile off. That's why I need you to do it. I need you to work out what's happening with her.'

'And you don't think she's having an affair? It'd be quite a disguise appearing in sweats and then taking them off for a fumble in the car before putting them back on again.'

'No, she's not, I know that; there's been nothing wrong with our bedroom activities,' he says. 'She's not hiding herself away from me in that sense—we're still very active. No, it's something else and with the money disappearing, she's being blackmailed about something but I don't know what.'

'What does she do, sir?' I ask

Again, he's looking around as if what he's about to tell me is some sort of breach of confidence. 'She works in the tourist industry,' and with that looks down into his coffee.

'Right?' I say, 'We're on Skye here. I dare say fifty percent plus of the people here work in the tourist industry. Could you be a little bit more specific?'

He raises his eyes and then mutters something about hotels and that sort of business. Apparently, she's on a few boards, helps organize the tourism in the area and places that look after accommodation.

'You got any names?' I say.

'You will be careful though,' he says. 'Don't look too close in case they find out.'

'This is my job, sir. It's what I do. I can look remarkably close without people knowing I'm looking so if you want me to do this, I need to know the detail and I can get on with it. If you want somebody to investigate and take your money, but not really investigate, I'm sure there's plenty of charlatans you can turn to. But you come to me and I will investigate.

He gives a smile but it's very reluctant. 'Okay,' he says and passes me some details about the places she works. I reckon I'll need to have a look at them.

'But one thing,' he says. 'She said to me, she's out tonight, she has to go. I know the jogging bottoms were freshly washed last night and her underwear too. Whatever she's doing, I think she'll be doing it tonight; the weather is meant to be quite good, if windy,' he says. 'It's usually on a good night that she goes so I do wonder if it's outdoors wherever it is she goes to.'

25

'And you're totally sure that she's not playing around?'

'I don't think she is.'

'And she hasn't been more attentive to you or completely less attentive or in any way asked for anything different, kinkier?'

The man shakes his head. 'And there is the money,' he says. 'The money is disappearing. It's a cash withdrawal and is done from all different branches and cash points, sometimes in a branch.'

'And what sort of money are we talking, sir?'

'Usually about five to six hundred pounds at a time,' he says. 'The account usually has three to four thousand in it, maybe turns over a thousand in a month. As I said it's like our play fund, emergency fund, things that we want to do, places we want to go, things like that, the nice things in life. The other accounts pay the bills. I generally don't look at it very much; it's just there—it floats. There's a standing order goes into it from mine and from hers. We've never had a problem; I only noticed when I looked at it.'

'Okay, sir,' I say, 'you're on and I start today.' I run down my fees with him before asking if he's got any more photographs of her. He takes a couple out of his wallet and I see that businesswoman again, a smiling face but behind it there seems to be a hard edge and if she works in tourism, to be fair, that could be a very good fit. At the back of four photographs, there's one of her on a beach. As I said before, she looked like she was in good shape, and it does look from this photograph, that she really is maintaining that shape.

'I take it she looks after herself well, sir,' to which he nods. 'Has she had any work done?' This is a bizarre question and if honest, has nothing to do with the job. It's just looking at her, and her age, I can't believe how good she looks.

'She likes to look good; she's had a few augmentations done,' he said and when I raise my eyes to look at him, he cups his hand in the chest area. 'It cost a bit,' he said, 'but it was worth it.'

I guess it was my fault but that was a little bit too much detail. I was thinking collagen injections and that, around the lips, things like that but obviously she's a woman that wants to look her best.

As he disappears, the man scans the café. If I had to ask anyone in here what they thought of him, I guess they'd say, 'That was a man who thought he was being watched.' Something's not sitting right but the man's money seems good and so I will have to disappoint Maggie. Susan's got enough on her plate and sometimes when jobs come, you have to take them because they don't turn up a second time. Hey, we all have bills to pay; Craigantlet doesn't moor for free.

Chapter Four

I have lunch that day with Maggie on board Craigantlet. I thought I was going to leave her to sleep through the afternoon but she rang me. She was back awake and she's probably going to sleep most of tonight without me if I'm going on stakeout so I thought the least I could do was spend some lunch time with her. In the afternoon, I make a phone call to Martha giving some details of my new client, of where his wife works, asking for a quick run through to see if anything strange has been happening on their account.

Martha's a woman I know from my past and she was used by people to dig into criminal activities, cover up things that weren't done so well. I cracked her case, and she would have been prosecuted but I kept her out of it because, to be honest, she was just a pawn being used. Martha's a big lady who worries about her size, doesn't like herself, and struggles at times with depression. But she's a genius upon the net. She can find information—she can track anything, here, there, and everywhere.

And I don't like people being used, so she's gone from a place of exploitation to being a paid advisor by me and she's happy. Well, as happy as Martha ever gets. She still worries she doesn't have enough friends and what people think of her but at least she's not being taken along for a ride at the same time.

I'll not hear back from Martha until tomorrow probably, so maybe I'll have time to look into things. I give Susan a call and decide to meet up for some coffee, a little bit of business chat. Then I'm going to spend an hour with her mother. That's one of the weird things at the moment having Susan work for me. Business over, we then get together like a small family and I have to switch off from being the boss. The day continues to be overcast and there's a little bit of rain on the boat but that's not stopping the tourists; they're everywhere and the place is as busy as it can be. The wind, however, is continuing. It's steady, and it's quite fresh but it's not blowing a hooley like it does in the winter. On the bright side, it will keep the midges away, the nasty little black, biting buggers that can ruin a holiday.

I meet Susan on the road between Kyle and Portree at a little stop which again has a very touristy feel to it. It's not a greasy spoon, but again is rather more elegant. There's cutlery, napkins, and delightful table mats on all the surfaces. The jam doesn't come in a plastic tub but instead comes in a little glass miniature.

Our brief work conversation takes about ten minutes. I find out that Susan thinks something's up again tonight and I believe she'll be on stakeout most of the night following the man. She tells me how the incident took place at the Fairy Pools and though she's been back several times, she can't find anything there. That's the most bizarre thing. She wonders is it just some sort of fraternity or little secret society because, apart from the rather bizarre sight, there doesn't seem to be anything untoward. She's struggling to find out anything about the man that she's tailing. She says that it might be something sexual; maybe this is a precursor but she's not sure.

I think she might be heavily influenced by certain happenings we saw in Stranraer, on the first case she was on with me. I keep pointing out to her that's the exception not the rule, but when you see people engaged in these rather funny, dress-up activities with certain overtones behind them, it's hard to shake it off from the mind.

I'm a little bit disappointed that I'm on stakeout tonight because I would have joined Susan to see what I could find out. But I drop Maggie back at Craigantlet. She gives me a kiss and tells me not to worry that she's quite happy taking out a book and a glass of red wine. With no nursing for a couple of weeks she's able to relax. She'll probably ring Kirsten for a chat later on. I say I'll be back but not to wait up for me. She laughs, telling me she expects love and attention on my return. She'll be lucky. She'll probably get some creaturely man start to snore his head off within five minutes.

I pick up a hire car before it closes and then make my way over to Kyle of Lochalsh. It's on the outskirts in a new belt and I find the house of Edward and Jenny Carnegie. There are two cars in the drive, so I reckon it's their home. It's quite awkward in daylight on a relentless day like this to be able to see what's going on. Getting up close is not always easy. But if you stay in someone's back garden, looking in a window, the neighbours who are looking down on you quite often frown at this. So, I'm a little bit stuck.

Jenny Carnegie comes out twice into the front garden. The first time she cuts some flowers, possibly for some vase inside and then heads back in. The second time she comes out, she seems to be performing some sort of Tai chi and I'm quite amazed at how supple the woman is for her years.

I make a note to myself that I seem to be shocked over and

over again at this woman and I'm trying to work out if I guessed wrong on her age. Is she actually a lot younger, but the face has just worn? But I know those eyes have seen things. You can disguise a lot, but you can't disguise the eyes. They say the eyes are the windows to the soul. And while that might work, we prefer to have evidence and go off solid facts. But you need to read a person in the moment. She's hiding something.

I picked up a sandwich at a garage earlier on and as I'm eating this at nearly ten o'clock, Jenny Carnegie leaves the house. I see her husband at the window, watching, and I note, she's dressed in her sweats. Her car is rather drab, which I find quite strange. I thought she'd be one to impress. But instead it's very sensible, not a BMW or Porsche but one of those middle-range cars. You expect a home of three or four to be driving practical, sensible, good mileage and easy to park but as far as I'm aware, they don't have kids. Certainly, no one ever mentioned. But Martha will come up with that for me.

We drive to Kyle and head into Skye where the roads are still reasonably busy, tourists making their way back to hotels, ready for some drinks for the evening. Although at ten o'clock, I'm sure a lot of them may even be heading towards bed. The breeze is still up and the light's incredibly good. But then again, at this time of year that's not surprising. In my mind there's a thought as to how Susan's getting on and that thought grows stronger as I realize we're driving out in the middle of Skye approaching from the west side. Surely, we couldn't be going to the same place.

She parks up at the Fairy Pools car park and I drive past before spinning around and coming in from the other direction to try and throw her off the fact she's being tailed. She doesn't seem to have noticed me. As I'm parking, she's taking a black duffel bag out of the boot of her car. She starts off down a path, nodding to some walkers who have just returned to the car park acting as if everything's perfectly normal. I notice there's a number of other cars here and part of me puts it down to the tourist season. But there's another side to things. Susan and her gathering that she's been watching. Did they all park in the same place? Maybe the cars belong to them.

In the middle of the night, tailing somebody down a forest path is easier than doing it within a city. I know I'm operating at a distance but can see her and she's excited. She's delighted to be going somewhere and she suddenly breaks off the path and we're not that far out from where the Fairy Pools are. I can hear the water and that's what makes me think we're close as she disappears.

The landscape's rocky, not forest and she must have disappeared behind some of these rocks, covered as they are in various shades of green. I can hear her mutter to herself. Following that direction in the wind, she appears over the top of a rock. In front of the woman are a number of what looks like long sheets of a very thin material. She's pulling off her sweatshirt and then dropping her sweatpants and I realize she's wearing the underwear her husband was talking about. She's cutting quite a figure but it's a rather bizarre place to be doing it. Then she starts to wrap the cloth around herself. It's barely covering anything, yet managing to cover all the essentials quite easily. She makes some adjustments and it seems she's got everything covered. That would indicate she's still got something on underneath. So clearly, she's not that risqué a person.

Dressed, she steps back to the path and I reach forward and instantly search the black bag that she's left in the secluded huddle. Inside I find makeup but no money—there's no cash. I don't want to stay too long in case I lose her in the dark. Everything in the bag says, 'I've come to dress up.' Realizing that, I quickly track back to the path and see her in the distance break off towards one of the pools. It's a little way off the path and around the side of it I can see quite a gathering. There must be at least ten men standing there, all dressed rather bizarrely in white. And then she starts to dance in front of them.

I'm not sure I can describe it as erotic. It's more like one of those fairies you see in a ballet. Although she does get close to them. I can't see who she's physically touching. Yes, her face, her hair on the cleverly designed outfit, might excite some men. But it doesn't seem to have that purpose. It's almost like it is ceremonial and I'm really rather confused. I need to get closer to see if I can work out what's going on between them. Then I catch a little glimpse of red hair. Keeping low, I crawl round, come up and touch someone on the shoulder, my hand flying over their mouth. The girl with the red hair spins round and Susan looks at me with eyes that say, *you bastard*. We both quickly turn back to watch the show.

The woman's getting really close to a lot of the men and I notice with a couple, she's saying things. With some of the others, she's behind them and I don't know if she speaks at all. But she continues to dance. The show seems to finish just after midnight. It's not fully dark; it's more like a twilight and I can easily see down the path. I tell Susan to keep an eye on her man and I'll speak to her tomorrow. I follow the woman back. Once again, she changes in the hollow she's found, getting back into her sweats and getting back to her car.

As she's about to step in, a man who's standing beside a Land Rover walks over, saying something to her. He's tall, maybe six feet four, and built very strongly. He places his hand on her shoulder, but she knocks it away, and he places his other hand on her other shoulder. Again, she knocks it down. He seems to be pleading with her about something but it's hard with the distance I'm at to make out what's being said. He then swears at her. I don't know if he's begging or he's shouting at her and exactly what way this relationship is working. But at one point, she's quite clearly staring him in the eye, telling him something he doesn't want to hear.

He slaps her across the cheek. It's a hard one, causing her head to turn and she rocks on her feet. He goes to apologize but she drives her knee right up into the middle of his legs and I watch him collapse to the ground. She gets in the car and drives off. I think about tailing her, but I've got a hunch that she's going home given the fact that she doesn't arrive in the next morning, but in the early hours of the morning. It would fit with the description of her by her husband. So, I stay and watch the man get into his Land Rover and follow him.

He returns to the north of the island, not far from Dunvegan Castle where he goes into a large house. As he gets out, I see lights come on in the house. It's two-storey, looking at it, but may easily have five or six bedrooms. A woman's at the front door as he walks towards it, wrapped up in a dressing gown and giving him hell. He tries to walk past her but she grabs him, forcing kisses on the side of his cheek. He shakes his head, pushes her off and goes inside. She sits down on the step and begins to cry.

I watch her for five minutes, feeling like a ghoul because she clearly needs someone to help her but it's my job to observe. And that's what I do until I see him come back. He puts a hand on her shoulder. She stands up and the next minute they're kissing strongly before going inside. I make a note of the address, get back in my car, and drive to Portree. Once there I go on the tender, head out to Craigantlet. Opening the little door, I step inside and see Maggie come through from the bunk room.

'You ready for bed?' she says. 'I've warmed it for you.' Something's gnawing at me and I need to think, what is going on here?

'Honestly, love,' I say, 'no; I'm going to stay here for a while. I need to chew something over.' She sits down on the seat at the side and calls me over, swinging her legs up onto the long wooden bench. And I don't miss them, trapping them in front of myself.

'Think away,' she says, 'I'll keep you warm while you do.'

I used to do this on my own. I used to come back and sit up all night thinking about cases, working out what's going on. And if I'm honest, I used to get lonely. I used to imagine that someone would be here for a night of passionate love but right now, just having somebody to hold me, this is all right. It's certainly better than coming home to a crying wife on the steps and getting kneed in the knackers by some dancing woman beside some local pools. Just what the hell is going on?

Chapter Five

The following morning is slightly overcast, a grey layer of cloud giving the morning a slightly chillier start. As I look around Portree harbour, there are still plenty of tourists on the move. I enjoy my breakfast with Maggie, who delicately avoids talking about the case. She can see there's something going on in my head—ideas, thoughts running around, and she stays quiet, occasionally passing a polite word about the day, but otherwise busying herself with the boat. Telling her I'll not be here for lunch, but I'll try and make dinner, I take the tender across, before driving to the small coffee house on the road between Kyle and Portree. Susan's there looking a little bleary-eyed. She has her hair tied up at the back, dressed in her jeans and t-shirt, a much more stylish affair than I can manage when I'm looking that casual.

As the tea arrives, I ask her, 'Did your man make it home safe then last night?'

'Mr Appleton went straight home; he didn't disappear anywhere else,' she says. 'He's not the most exciting man to follow.'

'He turns up at meetings beside pools in the middle of the night,' I say. 'What do you want?'

'His wife hasn't contacted me either,' she says, expecting a little bit of nosiness from her about what was happening. 'What about Mrs Carnegie? Anything exciting about her?'

I shake my head. 'I didn't even follow her back last night; instead I followed one of the other men,' and I relate the tale of the doorstep incident. 'Could you see what was happening last night?' I say to Susan. 'There's something else about that group. I think I might drop in on the local police and ask them about them, see if anybody knows about them or heard of them. But the messages being passed, I think they're there for a reason.'

'Messages?' says Susan, 'Sounds a bit far-fetched. Why would you go through all that trouble of doing that just to spread messages about?'

'It's an easy way to get everybody together. If you then want to turn around and say why you were there and not told the wife, you could always say that you're a bit embarrassed. It's not exactly a normal pursuit. If anyone sees you, tourists or whatever, then it's just one of those fun druidic dances. But I do know something's up. Stay on your man, get into what he's doing with this business.'

'Speaking of businesses,' says Susan, 'I was talking to the proprietor of the hotel I'm in. It's been the weirdest bit of being here. You've seen how busy the place is; there's tourists everywhere yet there's next to nobody in my hotel.'

'Really,' I say, 'is it nice enough? I mean is there something wrong with it?'

'No,' she says, 'it's perfectly good, nothing wrong with it; it just seems that nobody wants to stay. The owner joined me for breakfast this morning because there was no one else there. He sat down with me, gave me a whole story about how he's going to go out of business the way this is going.'

'Does he know why?' I ask.

Susan shakes her head, the red ponytail flapping behind her. 'But he mentioned a friend who's also struggling.'

'Get into that,' I say. 'Have a look at numbers here and your hotel and all the hotels, find out his friend's hotel, find out some other contact numbers. It just sounds a little bit strange. I want to see if there's a general problem.'

'Sure, Paddy,' she says, nodding. 'What are you doing today?'

'I think I'm going to take it easy,' I say, 'I'll drop in at the local police, see if I can have a word. Let them know I'm here because at the end of the day, this is all above board and I'll ask a bit about the gatherings at the Fairy Pools. I also might ask about the accommodation issue your proprietor has been having.'

I don't like walking in blind to a police station; I'm just a man who doesn't usually do that. It's far easier if you can find someone you either know or somebody else knows. I give Martha a ring, asking her to start looking at the hotels in the area and other accommodations, just generally going through the websites and things, see if there's anything strange she notes. I also ask her who currently works in and around Portree from the police force.

It takes a while to dig stuff up but she rings me back, saying that's unlikely I'm going to know any of them, except for possibly one person and that might not be a good person to talk to. He's a young lad and his father came from the province and I've worked with him. We had a few run-ins in our day but the man passed away two years ago. Whether the son's heard about me or not, I don't know, but I know other people on the force. They pass things along, people they didn't like, to their family, mentioning their annoyance at work with him and things like that. But I take a note of the name and number and call the station. The man's not working today, and I can't get a phone number off them, which is good practice and they're to be commended for it. But a call to Martha soon gets me an address and a phone number.

The call's picked up by a woman with a screaming kid in her hands. She then passes the phone on to a rough-sounding voice, but it's an accent I'm familiar with. The tone definitely comes from Northern Ireland but it's not as harsh as that of Belfast, instead having more of that country ring to it. It's not as soft as further south but it's still distinctly not from the city.

'How can I help you?' asks the man.

'Hi, my name's Paddy Smith. I'm in the area and I used to work with your father and I understand you're in the force as well. I'm just trying to find out a few things about the general area because I'm working as a private investigator and I was wanting to know if I could have a couple of minutes of your time just to run through some questions about the place. Not about you and your family or anything like that. Just about the place in general.'

'You worked with Dad?' he says, 'How long ago?'

'It would be about ten years since I worked with your father,' I say.

'He hardly ever talked about you, Smythe—wasn't too keen on you, as I recall,' he says.

'No, he wasn't and I'm not here to reminisce about how wonderful we were together because we weren't. I'm just trying to get some information, simple information, and I thought with the connection we have, I might get it better from you than walking in directly to the station.'

'You're the guy that lost the arm, aren't you?' he says.

'Yes' I am,' I say.

'He always felt for you about that, always was worried about how you got on afterwards. I'll give you my address,' the man says. 'Come over. I can't say I'll be a lot of use to you but if I'm any use at all and helps your business then that'll do, Mr Smythe.'

'Call me Paddy. I'll be over directly.'

Martin Kerr lives in a little estate, close to Kyle of Lochalsh. The estate itself looks fairly modern, one of the houses that often advertise three bedrooms but actually only have two and a half bedrooms. They come with neat drives, small gardens, and everything in decent working order for a family that's just about starting out. When I knock on the door, it's answered by a woman with a baby in her arms. She can only be in her early twenties and looks a little flustered. The youngster, he's probably between one and two, clamouring for attention and looking rather annoyed at this man who's arrived at the door.

She leads me through to the kitchen table, asking me if I want a coffee or tea to which I agree and then wait for her husband to arrive. The woman has closed-cropped hair and is dressed in a pair of jeans and a simple plain top. I'm not a large fan of short hair on a woman but I can see the reasons. Maggie seems to be brushing hers all day long but as much as I love it, if it were mine, I daresay I'd be hacked off at having to do that three or four times a day. After a couple of minutes, a man steps into the kitchen, kisses his wife on the cheek before walking over to me and offering a hand. I shake it and Martin Kerr sits down.

'I'm happy to talk to you,' he says, 'but I don't give out special information, anything that the force has that other people don't need to know.' He is staring at my arm or rather the one that's not there. 'Dad said you lost the whole lot right up to the top of your shoulder. Bomb blast, wasn't it?'

I nod my head. I didn't know where, just walking along. 'I lost one of your Dad's friends that night as well,' I say. 'It wasn't pretty. Back in times when things were pretty rough.'

'Yeah, he talks about it at times,' the man says, 'or he did. Cancer got him two years ago.'

'Sorry to hear that,' I say. 'We weren't the best buddies and we didn't always see eye to eye but John was a good officer. Is that your first kid?' I say, changing the subject.

Martin nods. 'Elaine's from here. That's why we're back here now. I lived briefly over in Northern Ireland when we first got married but came out here into the force. Just prefer it. Too many memories back there. Bit of bother.'

I'm fully aware of the bother that happened. There were a few words about corruption with his father, none of which I believe, but when something taints you it will taint you for a long time and I understand them moving away, 'But let's not dwell on that,' I say. 'I just want to know a little bit about Skye.' The man leans back in his chair, and lifts his palms up, ready for any questions.

'There's a little gathering that goes on, down at the Fairy Pools,' I say. 'I don't know if you guys are aware of it; some men come along dressed up in white. This woman dresses up in a number of veils. Nothing ridiculously erotic just quite druidic. Looks a bit strange. I was wondering if you knew anything about it.'

The man grins. 'That's been going on for a while now, seems to have built up. We get the odd tourists telling us about it but it's a druidic society. Nothing formal. There's nothing written down about the place they meet. But apparently, it blesses the land. And yeah, I did go down one night and she's not doing anything untoward. At first, I thought it was one of those dress-up, sexual-party things. But no, it's only plain old druidic rubbish.'

It's a candid answer and I'm sure they include the community so they're taking kindly to it. But I also get the feeling it wouldn't have been said if the man was in uniform.

'So, you had no issues with them at all?'

'None.' He says. 'Why do you ask?'

'I've trailed some people to this druidic performance, partners of people who think they're being cheated on. I'm not quite sure if they are involved in something else and I've got nothing to bring to you guys at the moment, nothing that says there's anything more untoward.' He nods and tells me that if anything does happen, I'm more than welcome to bring them to him. 'Thanks for that, I say, but there's something else; there's a couple of businesses, tourist hotels that don't seem to be doing very well at the moment. Do you know anything about that?'

'Whereabouts?' he says.

'Some are here in Kyle, some a little bit further inland—Skye, from what I've gathered.'

'I don't know anything about that,' he says. 'The only thing that's been a bit strange lately is the number of assaults we've had and not on tourists either. It's all been on locals, people left battered and bruised and they had no idea why they've been attacked. It's just something about it. It doesn't seem to be very random. It's attacking specific people but not like they've just been mugged in the dark. Usually, they've been followed and, in some cases, it seems to be from quite a distance out.'

'Anyone attacked in their home?'

'No,' he says, 'it's always been around and about.'

'Any of them link to these druid things?'

He shakes his head. 'We don't really have a list of who's at the druid stuff. I haven't really thought about that. Any particular reason why you think it is?'

'No,' I say, 'I'm just following up on these people, who are possibly playing around, and it's led to this druid gathering. I've got nothing to say any of the beatings are linked to that. In fact, it's the first I've heard of them when you've spoken about them—might not have anything to do with it.' The man nods but his eyes are telling a different story, and he's wondering what I'm on to.

'Anyway,' I say, 'time to hit the road, got a little bit of business tonight so I want to catch some shut-eye before I do.'

'All right.' he says. 'What's that about then?'

'Ah, just stalking, just making sure somebody's not going to a bed he shouldn't be.'

The man laughs, 'Well, good luck to you on that. I guess it pays the bills.'

'It does,' I say. 'And all the best to your family there.' As he takes me to the door, his wife joins him and I look back to see the three of them, the baby huddled between the two of them and I think about things I never had. Having Maggie now is quite something but we're never going to be like that. My days with kids are gone and now when I see how happy people can be, I do feel I've missed out. But then I take the other cases and see how they've fallen apart and thank God that I never got married and started a family. *You pays your money and takes your choice in this life.* And then you get what you get.

I'm pretty morbid as I drive back, pondering on the life I could have had, until I take the tender across to the boat. I see the smiling face of the brunette woman walking around Craigantlet with her shorts and t-shirt. As I climb aboard and give her a hug, I tell her I'm going down below for a sleep. 'I'll be on stakeout tonight,' I say.

'So, I won't be seeing you then probably until the morning.' said Maggie.

'True,' I say. 'By the time I get up, eat something and then I go, I'm hardly going to see you. Sorry about that.' As I make my way below deck, I hear Maggie following me down and I walk through to the bunk, start to take my top off and then my trousers before climbing in. As I lie up against this side of the boat, a preferred position, to look at the blank wall, I hear somebody else in the room, my cover gets thrown back and a pair of arms enfold me, pulling me close. I think about settling down, enjoying this and going to sleep except the lack of clothing tells me that Maggie's not up for sleep.

'I need sleep, I say, 'I've got a stakeout tonight.'

There's a smack at my bottom. 'And I need something else, Mr Smythe, so shut up. When I'm done with you, you'll have no problem sleeping.' I laugh and roll over. These are definitely better days than when I worked alone.

Chapter Six

It is stuffy in the car, so I step outside and then look at the house where I observed the fight between the man and the woman the night before. I hope tonight to tail him, see what else I can find out about him, but he seems to be a home bird, not going anywhere. I elect to get closer to the house to see if I can hear anything but this won't be easy until the later hours. I decide I can't wait that long, really not looking forward to the idea of an entire night hunkered down in this car. The man's doing nothing. Maybe the only time he does something interesting is when he heads to those Fairy Pools. So, I decide to make my way up in the last of the daylight but it's still here after eleven o'clock at night.

It's one of the funny things about being this far north in Scotland and in the height of the summer, there's almost a twilight and not a night and I have to be extra careful as I approach the house. I can hear a TV on inside. I'm keeping low underneath the windows and listening out for voices but there's nothing. I keep away from the front door and at the back, I make my way over to a small shed and sit behind it, looking out occasionally, trying to find the lay of the land.

There's an upstairs light on, which looks like the bathroom while downstairs there appears to only be a light from the front, possibly the lounge. The upstairs light switches off and another figure appears in the lounge. I can see through from the rear of the house that the kitchen leads through to it, but it's only a small part of lounge I can see. The wife or partner of the man, also the woman I saw before on the doorstep, is wearing a dressing gown and appears to speak to the man for a while. It's all very normal and then suddenly she shakes. I can't make out the words exactly but she storms off upstairs, a light goes on in the bedroom before the lights in the lounge switch off, and soon the whole house is in the dark. It's barely gotten to midnight and it looks like my stakeout is a bust.

On my way back to the car, I get inside and wonder what to do, I pick up my mobile, send a text to Susan to see how she's getting on with her stakeout. She tells me that the woman's out and about currently in town, at a small bar but she appears to be talking to some friends, Susan can't get close enough to hear the conversation, but she says it doesn't look like anything serious.

This is the point where I should think Maggie's stuck in the boat—let's just go back and have a good night cuddled up there before coming back to work in the morning. But something's bothering me about this woman that Susan's following, and I decide to tail her. I also might get a chance to see how good Susan is at her job. So, I don't tell Susan I'm coming over, but drive to the bar which Susan advised was on the main street in Portree and sits slightly behind the others. The close nature and winding roads of Portree means it's easy to park up somewhere and wander around—lots of nooks and crannies to dive into if you don't want to be seen.

As I approach the bar, I tiptoe past the window and look inside. Sure enough, there's the woman, chatting away with her friends and there's Susan in the corner, looking like some sort of nerd with a large book out in front of her. She has her red hair tied up in pigtails and there's a backpack sitting beside her. Cleverly there's no tent with the backpack which means she's either staying at the hostel or she's already camped out somewhere.

I hang around outside, waiting to see any developments and it's half an hour before the woman leaves with her friends. They say goodbye and kiss on the cheek before she gets into her car and drives back to the Kyle of Lochalsh. I tail behind Susan and watch as she keeps an eye on the woman going into her house. Susan then waits for an hour and sees all the lights in the house off before calling it a night.

It's only by chance I'm still here and it's an hour later. I had asked Martha for some details but I had decided to read them here rather than back on Craigantlet. I sit in the car and scan through what she had found out about the area. It's not a lot at the moment, just some information about how the druid society wasn't that keen on this display at the Fairy Pools, calling them not a proper branch, whatever that means. With a casual eye, I spot the bathroom light coming on and I don't think much of it as it disappears two minutes later. But two minutes after that, the car the woman drove home in is now fired up and she's racing off. Throwing the details I was looking at on the seat beside me, I tail her at a reasonable distance given it's night time and there's next to nobody else about.

I see her drive back over the bridge into Skye again. She's not difficult to follow and I doubt she thinks somebody's on her but she ends up driving through the gates of what seems like a large estate. I park the car some way off before returning and make my way close to the driveway of the large house. It's in darkness but her car is outside.

Taking a scan of the outside, it appears to be reasonably deserted, so I decide to try and chance my luck at open doors. Given she's coming in the middle of the night and without lights on, I reckon something might have been left open for her. Making my way around the back of the building, I find a door which leads inside to a back passage. The house I'm standing in is large by any modern standards and there's three floors. It looks like some sort of Grand Victorian style but the furnishings are modern.

There's hardly a sound as I make my way through the ground floor finding a kitchen, a working studio, a lounge area, and a games room. The next floor seems to be office space, more lounges, a TV room but again there's no one about. As I make my way up to the final stairs, I start to hear voices. There's laughter, giggling and then little conceits being made, whispers in the dark. As I pass one room, I can tell that she's up to something with either a gent or a woman. I don't hear any other voices, just her own and she's out of breath, telling someone just how good he is. I take a quick tour of the rest of the top floor finding only bedrooms but make my way into one that has a wall which connects with the room she's gone into from which I can hear the voices.

I spend the next hour holed up against the wall, listening to two people enjoying themselves and each other. It's not exactly the greatest time when you're a private investigator. You don't learn much and some ways you just feel disappointed you're not off with your own beloved having a similar sort of night. But it's all part of the job and I listen to hear if I can pick up any little pieces that are given away in the dark. There's nothing; it seems to be purely about what's going on in the room. After an hour, I hear her say that she's going downstairs for a drink. The door opens and I believe she leaves and a man's voice shouts—he's coming too. I wait until I hear them move down the stairs before exiting my room and following them down. They make it all the way to the ground floor, the lights now on in the house and as I creep by the kitchen, I hear her start to talk.

'Has she given it yet? It's about time you back down,' says the woman.

'Patience, you're as feisty out of the bedroom as you are in it.' says the man. 'You have to have patience in the long run here; things are proceeding.'

'You always tell me patience,' she says. 'I come over here, give you all you're looking for and you tell me patience. When am I coming over here to stay?' There's an anger in the woman's voice but it also sounds like she's baiting the man.

'You enjoy being here as much as anyone,' he says. 'I don't have to invite you over—you just appear.' He laughs and I hear them move closer together. There's a slap and a hand on someone's backside, some wet kissing, a different sound, and then the tap comes on.

'You can pour me a glass, too,' the man says. 'Look at me I'm dripping.'

'You didn't think someone like me would last this long, did you?' she says.

'For a woman of your age, you have the bearing of a twenty-year-old.'

There's a slap and suddenly her voice is cool and very, very earnest, 'Never refer to me as a woman of my age.' she says.

'Why? I like something a bit mature.' Again, another slap.

There's an awkward silence before she breaks it.

'Tomorrow night,' she says, 'are you all set?' The man agrees. 'Good, I don't want any cock-ups; make sure they're all there. Have they sorted out our problem?'

'It's in the hand,' says the man. 'He's being made to understand and if he doesn't, well, that's when we'll take more decisive action.'

'And what sort of action would that be?' she says.

'We'll bury him if we have to. You know I would do anything for you.' I then hear hands being placed on the woman. Sounds like there's a bit of rough and tumble and they're off again. I half listen in, mostly to work out when they're finished but it takes another half an hour before they roll out of the kitchen and into the hallway. I have to stay tucked away, peering out very reluctantly from my spot in the room next to the kitchen but I see two pair of buttocks before they disappear back up the stairs.

It is isn't long before she's returning, clothes over her arm and her shoes held in her hand. She comes down, back into the kitchen and I hear more water being poured out. I sneak my way past, realising that the upstairs light had been switched off. As I take a glance in the kitchen, I see her standing at the sink, splashing water over her entire body, washing herself. I make my way back outside and sure enough, five minutes later she's out, fully dressed, and the car's driving off. I tail her back to her house at four in the morning; she goes back inside. At five, I call it a night and head back over to my boat, taking the tender to it. Maggie's awake as I come onboard.

'Good evening, was it?'

'Yes,' I say, 'I watched your daughter come up short on her cover before I tailed the woman to her house and listened to two people having a lot of fun throughout an entire evening.' Maggie raises her eyebrows, 'Yes, that sort of fun. But I also know something is up and I know something untoward's being done. I just haven't got a clue what at the moment but the first thing I'm going to do in the morning is wake your daughter up and give her a row for not staying on our tail long enough.'

'Take it easy', says Maggie. 'She's only new at this and she's been out tailing her round for the last lot of nights.'

'I know, but she needs to learn.'

'Anyway, what's your plans now?' says Maggie.

'I thought I'd go to sleep. I'm absolutely shattered. Have you had much sleep last night?'

Maggie shakes her head, 'The trouble with sleeping with you,' she says, 'is I don't sleep properly then when it comes to my own turn.' I take her hand, lead her through to the bunk but there's no anticipation or excitement. We both simply strip off, go inside the bed and within a minute I can hear her lightly snoring behind me. I grab her arm, wrap it around my waist and lie there in the dark thinking: *Who were they talking about in the kitchen? Who's driving who in this endeavour? And why was it so easy to tail her? And how lightly does her husband sleep when she makes her way back in then disappears out before coming back again.* He obviously doesn't sleep light at all maybe I'll ask him just what he saw the other previous night. There's clearly something going on and I need to get a handle on it. I know she's out tomorrow night; she mentioned about meeting again but I think I'll try and track her and approach her, do some one-to-one questioning. I think I'll do it so that it leaves Susan still undercover.

Chapter Seven

We get about four hours sleep before I inform Maggie that I need to get up and going again. A quick text to Susan tells me that she's not made it out of her hotel yet. I ask her why she's not watching her tail; she says that the woman never leaves the house before eleven. It's nice she doesn't get overexcited. I tell her I'll meet her for a bacon roll once I get a chance to leave the boat. Maggie asks if she can come with me. I think about this, but then my plan was probably to meet the woman today in some regards. It might look good to have someone with me so we look the type simply up on holiday. So, I agree, and we take the tender together back over to the car in Portree. I drive and stop off at a local cafe, grabbing a quick bacon roll and am joined shortly by Susan.

'So where were you last night?' I say. Susan looks at me incredulously.

'I was on my tail; she went to the bar and then she went home.'

'That she did,' I say, 'but is that all she did?' Susan raises her eyebrows.

'Paddy was watching them have sex last night,' says Maggie and begins to laugh at Susan's shocked face. I, however, am not laughing.

'You didn't stay on your tail long enough; you didn't give it time to see what else she would be doing. I don't know if she's been up on any other nights; how long have you stayed up there on those?' I ask.

'Usually to two in the morning, maybe three,' says Susan. 'She's never gone out before.'

'Well, she did last night', says Maggie, 'and from what Paddy said, it would have been a heck of a show.'

The tone's a little light for my liking, but it is awkward to tick off my working partner when her mother is sitting right beside me. 'Keep an eye on her today,' I say, 'but don't be surprised if you see me. I intend to make an approach today, try and find out something from her, but I want you to stay in the shadows. Once I've seen her, it's going to be much harder for me to tail her but not you. And don't forget to change up your hair, she saw the red pigtails last night; use one of the wigs. Susan looks at me with pleading eyes, I know it's because she's very fond of her red hair, sees it as something that defines her, but she's undercover—the last thing she needs to be is defined.

'Be a good looking brunette like your mother,' says Maggie and again laughs.

'Time we got going,' I say. 'Go to her house, tail, tell me where she heads for and we'll see if we can accidentally bump into her.'

Susan disappears and I sit with my phone contacting Martha. I give the address that I was out at last night and ask for information about the man that lives there. She sends back information about our previous attendee at the Fairy Pools. The man's name is James McAvoy, and he's involved in a lot of the youth hostelling around the area. It seems that he has various sites, different farms, as well as running his own farming business. From what Martha can tell, the youth hostelling is what's keeping the farm going as it seems to be losing money hand over fist. According to government data, he's married to Elin McAvoy and has birth certificates for two kids. But beyond that, there's not a lot; she couldn't reach into the bank account and she's wanting to know how much more I need to know. I tell her to keep digging on all fronts, including our female friend Jenny Carnegie, as she seems to be one of the main drivers in this.

I sit with Maggie for another hour before we get a phone call. Susan advises that the woman has gotten into the car and headed for the beach. She's made her way over to the west side of Skye.

'I was heading down a little trail,' Susan says, 'and am now watching her putting suntan lotion—on what is an extremely quiet beach.'

I get a GPS readout from her phone, and together we head off. We find the spot on the west side of the isle and realize just how remote it is. The sun is absolutely blazing and I swear it must be around about twenty-five to twenty-six degrees as Scotland enjoys some of its best summer weather in a long time. I'm beginning to sweat and it's not really the sort of weather I enjoy, but Maggie seems more at home.

'What's your plan?' she whispers in my ear, despite the fact we're so far away from the woman she could never hear us.

'Well, what's she doing at the moment?' I say.

'Can't see,' says Maggie, and so I hand her a pair of binoculars from the backpack. 'Blimey, she's just sunbathing. And by the way, did you say you saw her al fresco last night?'

'Yes, she was with her lover and I passed by the kitchen and caught a glimpse of her.'

54

'It's no wonder you're tailing her then. Look at that! I know your game, sunshine.' She digs an elbow into me and I give a smirk but I don't like the insinuation. When you tend to creep around, spying on people who are cheating, you tend to see all sorts of things. 'So how are you going to talk to her?' says Maggie.

'We are,' I say. 'We're going down there to do a bit of sunbathing.'

Maggie looks at me. 'But I haven't got a swimsuit,' she says. 'I've got no bikini or anything.'

'Indeed, I haven't got a lot with me either, we'll just have to make do.' Before she can argue, I put the binoculars back in the car, take her hand, and we make our way down to the beach, which involves coming down from some rocks and I reckon Susan's watching from the far side. If she's got half a clue, she's got a camera right as well.

I tell Maggie just to act like we're dying for a bit of fun on the beach, not to stare at the woman too much. In fairness, she plays her part, taking my hand as we run on, and then we look surprised at someone there. The woman at first ignores us, lying in the sun, bronzing herself in a black bikini with not an awful lot to it and I think that's annoying Maggie. But we walk along past the woman before I stop her, and I take off my coat. I strip down to my pants and then lie down on the sand, suggesting Maggie should join me. She's very self-conscious as she removes her clothing down to her underwear before lying down beside me. I roll over with my back to the woman and pretend to whisper something in Maggie's ear as I run my hand across her stomach.

'Is she looking?' I whisper.

'Yes,' says Maggie. 'She's got her eye on us at the moment.'

Maggie puts her hand on my buttocks.

'That's it.' I say. Maggie plants a kiss on me and her hand starts to run up and down my back and I wonder just how far she's going to take this. But she gives my backside a little smack. I feel I need to warn her.

'Easy, we're here to observe her, not just get carried away.'

'Look,' she whispers in my ear, 'you bring me down here, you make me wear my underwear, while you sit there telling me you're going to study some stunner. You'll get what you're given, mister.' She slaps me again on the backside. I start to tickle her and soon we're falling over each other, with a laugh. As we roll, I notice the woman, now sitting up. I hope she doesn't stare at us but she keeps flicking her head around, looking for us, seeing what we're up to. After a couple of minutes, I sit up too, arm around Maggie.

'Sorry, we got a bit carried away. Did we disturb you? It's just we've come to this beach the last couple of days and no one's been here.'

The woman turns with a smile, 'Not a problem; it's always good to see people enjoying each other.' With that, she turns back and lies down again.

'Hang on a minute,' I say. 'I've seen you before somewhere, haven't I?'

The woman sits up like a shot, turning around, 'Have you?' she says. 'I doubt it, although you may have seen me in around Skye. I do live and work here.'

'No, no, where were we?' I say to Maggie. 'Where were we, Maggie? What did we see, it was those druid people, wasn't it?'

I can see the nervousness in the woman's face. 'Yes,' says Maggie, 'you were dancing. We saw her dancing, didn't we? You've got a lovely turn on you, and you've got the figure for it.'

'Well, we all have to stay in tune with nature, don't we?' she says, 'and that's just me giving back to it.'

'Really,' I say, 'that quite interests us. We've been to Stonehenge and that before, but not here.' I get up hoping Maggie will follow my lead to sit on one side of the woman. Maggie comes over joining me, sitting on the other side so Jenny Carnegie has to turn her head left and right. Behind the woman is her bag which is partly lying open.

'Where were we last time, Maggie?' I say.

'We're down in Cornwall,' says Maggie, 'if I remember right. They had all those Morris dancers as well.' she says. 'Why do you wear that stuff when you're dancing?'

The woman turns and looks at Maggie and starts detailing about the dress, and how the different parts come together and how it's part of a ritual. I'm completely ignoring her and instead I've leant back slightly staring inside the bag. I can see a phone and I'm wondering if it's possible to get and take it away. Maggie continues to chat, talking more and more about druidic events she's been at, which is all news to me, especially as she keeps saying I was there with her. But as the woman replies and engages in the conversation, I lie back, lean over with my hand, and lift the phone out of the bag, putting it behind me. I sit up just as the woman turns back to me.

'And what do you get out of these experiences you've been to?' asks the woman.

'A sense of enlightenment,' I say. 'I always think it's good to touch nature.'

'Have you been to any riskier ones?' she says.

'Riskier? What do you mean exactly?'

'The ones that like to catch you doing the ceremonies with a lot less clothes,' she says.

'Yes, I have. I find them quite shocking in some ways,' I say, 'That took Maggie a little bit of getting used to, running around in the buff.'

The woman's head flicks back to Maggie and she looks at her and says, 'Yes, I remember the first time I did it' and starts off on some diatribe about being close to nature without anything on. As the woman's head is turned away, I indicate to Maggie that I need to get to the car.

'And also the water,' says Maggie. 'I love the water. I think you can feel a lot closer in it. What's the water like round here?' she says, and in my head, all I can think is salty, cold. 'Do you feel any vibrations through it, any sense,' says Maggie, and the woman looks at her not comprehending what she means. Maggie stands up, 'Come, I'll show you.' And with that, she takes the woman's hand, who stands up and together they walk out towards the sea. Maggie then flicks her head back and says, 'Oh, Paddy, go get us some towels, I think I left them in the car.' And with that, I watch the pair of them, walking out to the sea.

If it wasn't for this blasted phone, I'd have been able to sit there and enjoy that but instead I walk back up to the car. Once inside, I phone Hans and tell him I need him to break into a phone and blooming quick. I pull out the SD card from the phone, slip it into a little device I have in the back. It's basically a card reader but it connects through to Hans. He's operating the interrogation of it. While he's doing that, I have the boot open and start to put towels up on top of the car roof and then step back and take a drink of water from a large bottle, all in good sight of the woman so it doesn't look like I'm doing anything in the car. But I need not have worried as Maggie's got her standing in the sea facing out towards the open water and then going up and down in it, no doubt trying to tap into something.

It takes Hans about three minutes before he texts me back and says, 'All done.' I slip the card back inside the phone, put the battery in, and set it up again, checking it to make sure that it's come back home with the right time and date. With towels over my shoulder, I make my way back down to the beach, lie down at my previous spot, and making sure the girls are still looking out to sea, drop the phone back into the bag.

About a minute later, the girls return, and I hold out some towels. Maggie looks at me with eyes that say, *I know you're enjoying this*, so I just smile and ask if they felt anything when they were out there. Jenny says *yes* and she starts telling me about the waves and ripples of water that reached inside of her, how she felt she was almost a fish. I smile broadly. I watch Maggie shiver a bit in the cold. The sun may be up, but there's still a breeze and she's just come from water that's probably around thirteen degrees, so she'll feel chilled for a bit. I let her sit down in front of me and start drying her.

'This is Jenny, by the way,' says Maggie. The woman gets up on her knees as she dries herself, telling me how she thinks she's found someone in Maggie who she can relate with, 'A soul sister,' she says. I spend another half an hour chatting about how nature connects through the water, before I say to Maggie that we have to run, otherwise we'll miss our dinner reservation. I say goodbye and Jenny gets up to hug us both, before lying back down again on the sand, soaking up some more sunshine.

We make our way back up to the car, put the towels away, and dress. Once inside the car, Maggie turns to me and says, 'Do all your stakeouts go like this? I can see why you enjoy the job.'

I give her a snarky look and advise her that I have got the details of her phone. 'And well played you,' I say; 'you're like a natural.'

She turns and looks to me quite seriously. 'I was shaking inside. And I saw your eyes when we went to the water. I think this was all a ruse just to get me in my underwear out in that water.'

'All strictly professional work.'

'Liar,' she says, reaches forward, puts her arms around me and gives me a long kiss. When she breaks off, she sits back and simply looks at me.

'What?' I say.

'Let's do it again,' she says, 'but next time, don't bring the hot woman and let's just enjoy that beach together.' I smile and start the car driving away before it dawns on me—it'll probably be another couple of weeks before I get the chance to do that and Maggie will be back off holiday, working again. *I hate work*.

Chapter Eight

S omething's bothering me as I'm about to set out for a night of watching. I'll be stuck in the car again, waiting to see where Jenny Carnegie goes but I'm beginning to think she's more than important in this case. She could be the centre of something. Martha's got the details that Hans took off the mobile phone and she's working through them. At the moment, all I know is there's a lot of contracts and contacts around the hospitality industry, namely hotels, guest houses, places to book up anything of a reasonable size. Martha said there were also calendar dates of people that needed visited or put down as basic, simple meetings. But even looking over the last couple of days, she hasn't been to any of these meetings and it makes me wonder who has.

I decide to meet up with Susan again because I'm beginning to think that this could get a little bit stickier, a few more rogue elements involved. I might have trained her well and how to stay out of things, but I just want to be sure that she's safe. Two of us together gives less opportunity to be dispatched or done away within the night. I leave Maggie on Craigantlet, take the tender across, jump in the car and meet up with Susan just outside Kyle of Lochalsh. I dump my car, getting into her hire car and soon we're sitting outside the house.

Jenny Carnegie's car is in the drive and it's about eleven o'clock when she comes out to get into it. Her husband's following her and there's a blazing row going on. I notice her packing some bags, and she seems to be telling him that she's off. Having seen what she gets up to, I'm not surprised but I also wonder if this is a bit of a show. She's even standing on the doorstep, ready to drive away in her sweats, almost looking like she's going out for a jog more than anything else.

We start to tail her and I tell Susan where she can expect to go, getting to the estate house she was in before probably, maybe up for another night of passion. Susan raises an eye, and she's probably wondering how somebody in their forties can have a night of passion, in a way that young people do. Once you've passed twenty-five, you're basically gone, aren't you? Or at least that's how they see it; my work tells me different.

But that's not the way she goes anyway. Instead Jenny Carnegie seems to be heading for the Fairy Pools. She drives to the car park, where I first followed her and gets out of the car, the light still strong enough and we can see quite clearly all around. This means we have to stay at a distance. She finds her favourite haunt where she begins to change. Once again, she puts on the fancy cloths and comes out, looking like some goddess of old, a sacrifice or a dancing nymph, which is quite a transformation for a woman of her age.

While we track her, she makes her way to the Fairy Pool where she gathered at before, just above the water. She joins a group of men, all dressed in white standing in a circle but this time, I can see someone else on the far side of the water. They look like tourists standing with their binoculars as she dances about.

Once again, I see her get close to the men whispering

something in their ear before dancing off again. It's as before and I'm struggling to lip-read because she seems to have her back constantly to me, whispering up close to the men's ears. The charade seems to go on for at least twenty minutes and I see the general public still watching.

'This is going on longer than last time,' says Susan and I can see she's getting edgy. She still hasn't learned that skill of an investigator to just sit and be quiet and happy. But she is right. This dance is longer than last time and it seems to be very repetitive, like she got to the end of it and didn't know what to do and started again. I look across the pool and see that there's still another three men there, standing, watching her dance about. They're young, in their twenties, tourists, and the occasional binocular is still going up. They seem to be enjoying what she's doing; there's laughs, and jokes about it. But eventually, they move off, bored eventually of this dancing woman.

As soon as they're clear, I see her stop dancing and a man dressed in white walks forward. The men put their hoods up covering their faces and I wonder what's going to happen because this is the first time I've seen the men move out of the circle to come towards her. Normally, they stand and wait until dismissed. The man walking towards her at the moment, although I cannot see his face, stands about six feet four. He seems strong and reaches out, grabbing her wrist. He turns to the rest of them, not saying a word but holding her, dragging her around the circle in front of the men. The men close in and it's hard to see what's going on, especially as Susan has taken the binoculars off me and is keeping watch. There's a lot of commotion and the woman seems to be being pushed back and forward.

Susan whispers under her breath, 'Paddy, for God's sake, what are they doing?' and hands me the binoculars. When I focus in, I see that the cloths from her clothing have been ripped and thrown into the air. One of the men slaps her across the face, and as she falls to the ground, she's caught by the others. She's left now in her underwear, and they close round again, making it difficult to see exactly what they're doing. And then I see one of the men hold his hand over her mouth and others come up one by one. It's too dark to see exactly what they're doing; it's too far a distance and there's too many of them with their backs to me but whatever it is, she's not enjoying it. After a couple of minutes of this, the abuse seems to get more physical, with several men slapping her around the face.

'God sake, Paddy, we have to do something,' says Susan. 'We need to get her out of there.'

'Susan, I know what you're thinking, and you're right, we need to get her out of there, but how?'

'Distract them? Run off with her?'

'How do we get in? There's at least ten to twelve of them. Look at the size of some of them. Disturb them now and let them know we're here? They'll come for us and end us.'

'Then we need to phone the police.'

'Not at the moment—she's alive,' I say. 'If they take her from here, we could follow them, work out where they're going. I also don't like this; something doesn't feel right.'

'But you were with her today. What happens if you were spotted at the scene? What happens if they noticed you?'

'I doubt it,' I say, and I do doubt it. I know Maggie was with me and I know that sometimes she can get me distracted. But I was good today. I was looking around, I had my work head on, and I didn't see anyone. I grab Susan's arm, holding her because she looks like she's about to run forward and shake. 'No,' I say.

'But, Paddy, we have to do something.'

But before the debate rages any further, the circle breaks and the woman is lying on the ground. Susan begins to move and I hold her tight.

'She's dead, Paddy,' she says; 'she's dead.'

I shake my head. 'She's not dead; look at her—she's still breathing. They've broken off for a reason.'

And as if on cue, the largest of the men steps forward, picks the woman up and throws her over his shoulder and turns to walk away. One of the other men steps forward with a blanket and throws it over, which covers her bare behind that was sticking out. I'm not quite sure how this is helping their cause. They're a load of men marching along in white, looking like druids and now have a woman over one of their shoulders with a blanket around her, instead of being carried in her underwear. I guess it's an adjustment that might help but it seems a little bit strange.

The men depart, heading back towards the car park that we parked in. I see them move into the area like Jenny Carnegie did, a place where she got dressed. These are places off to the side, easy to get into, relatively hidden, and easy to get back from. The men are all dressed as anybody would: Corduroy trousers, shirts, t-shirts, jumpers. But Jenny isn't; she's still got the blanket wrapped around her.

They then walk to the car park, some of them getting in different cars but I notice one person getting into Jenny's. Jenny is placed in the car passenger seat and they drive off. As they exit the car park, I notice that some go left, but only a few go right, including Jenny's car, and I indicate to Susan that we need to hurry.

We have to stay a little way back as there are three cars up ahead. We're fortunate that they don't go very far before turning off a small road which heads out towards the sea. The track itself comes up near to a cliff edge and it's here that they stop.

I leave Susan in the car waiting to turn it on as quick as she can if needs be, and I steal up closer. It's not that easy due to the terrain around me, which tends to be a lot of grass but I can see them pushing her car now off the road onto a little track that leads perilously close to the cliff edge. The path slopes down towards it and the car is parked. They take Jenny out, moving her into the front seat before removing the blanket. One of the cars drives off, leaving only one man standing beside Jenny's car and another car waiting for him.

He reaches inside, I think he's let go of the hand brake. He turns and then throws a match into the back of the car. Maybe he wants it to look as the car had something go wrong with it though I'm not quite sure how that works, but there's flames leaping up in the back seat. The man has run for the car his friend is waiting in and they drive off at pace. Jenny's car has become yellow, the back seats ablaze but even more seriously, it starts to roll forward. What's worse is I don't think I'm going to get there.

I start running immediately, but as I perceive it with the speed of the car building up, there's no way I'm going to reach it before the cliff edge. That doesn't mean I'm not going to try. And as I sprint forward, my lungs fighting for more air, I try not to stare too hard, but focus on my running. Time seems to become non-linear and it's like I live in the moment racing as hard as I can. The car is only six feet from the cliff edge when

I reach it and pull open the door.

When I reach in, I place my hand on the woman's shoulder and pull her as hard as I can. She has to move out and I have to grip her hand hard. I see her feet get caught in the car and it starts to drag me. I can feel the flames, and one of the back windows bursts, smashed by the heat. Fortunately, her foot starts to loosen and together we roll away to one side as the car pitches off the top of the cliff. It tumbles down a couple of minor ledges and then disappears off. I haven't seen the drop beyond but I imagined it to be sheer, maybe thirty feet down to the sea. Jenny Carnegie's barely moving, and I looked down to see if there's any more permanent damage. She seems to be cut around the legs, probably from when I tried to get her out. There's bruising to the right of her face, possibly from some of the slapping and beating she took earlier. I hear a car pulling along that's right behind me, and as I look up, I'm relieved to see it's ours. Getting first to my knees, I pull Jenny up, place my shoulder into her midriff and lift her as I stand, my one arm over her.

'Susan, open the back door,' I say, making the couple of steps towards our car, dropping Jenny into the backseat. Closing up, I get inside, and I tell Susan to drive.

'Where?' she asks, and I tell her the opposite direction to which the other cars disappeared.

'But where do we go? Do we drive around Skye aimlessly? Do you think they saw us?'

'Did they see me going to the car?'

'I don't know, Paddy, possibly not,' she says. 'They certainly didn't come back. Surely if they had seen you, they'd have watched.'

I tend to agree. 'In that case, go to Portree. We're going to take her aboard Craigantlet, keep her there.'

'Mom's going to be chuffed. You bring a woman in her underwear back to her love nest on the boat. You really know how to show a woman a great holiday.'

I laugh and I see Susan shaking a little while she's driving. The joke was forced, intended to help her but I'm not sure it did. She seems rather nervous as we pull into Portree. Getting close to the tender, I tell her we're going to have to carry the woman in and borrow Susan's coat in the meantime. Together, the three of us, Jenny Carnegie, now with a coat around her and no longer in simply her underwear, make our way to the tender, one of Jenny's arms is around me and one around Susan and if anyone sees us or asks, I'm basically going to tell them she's had a skin full, but I'd rather they didn't. I jump into the tender and the quiet motor putts its way across to Craigantlet. As we arrive, Maggie comes on deck.

'Don't say anything; just get her inside and get her to the bunk. Quiet as we can.' It's a bit of a lift to get her up onto the boat as Jenny is still not making any sounds. Thankfully, I've got two women with me which makes it easier to heave Jenny inside and place her on the bunk. Maggie gives her a quick once over while I sit inside the main cabin with Susan. After a while, she comes back out, disappears in with her first aid kit before coming out again ten minutes later.

'It's a good job she's unconscious,' says Maggie. 'If I thought you were bringing a fully aware woman in her underwear to our bedroom, I'd have words to say.'

It's funny how mom and daughter both have that jokey aspect when the pressure's on. Maybe the younger one learnt it from the elder, but it's not a bad thing. Maggie says that Jenny Carnegie's in okay shape, just a bit banged and bruised, nothing broken. But she says she's been sedated in some way and that's why she's unresponsive.

'She stays here until she wakes up and we find out what's going on. You okay looking after her, Maggie? I need to get Susan back.'

'Not only do you bring this woman in wearing next to nothing, but you also want me to take care of her.'

It's not a great joke, but at least it keeps the atmosphere from getting a lot more serious. But I notice as Susan goes to leave, Maggie grabs hold of her, hugs her tight, telling her to be careful. I never really told her mother enough about her last escapade, the bit where Susan and I got caught and how she was close to being tortured, tortured in a very bad way. Susan said we shouldn't tell her and she is right, but Maggie's got a sense of things. As I go to step out of the cabin, she grabs my single arm, pulling me back. 'Careful,' she says, 'it sounds like it's getting very hot.'

'It is,' I say, 'but something's wrong with this, something in my gut says it's wrong but don't leave the boat. You were with me today; if we were being watched, they know you too.'

But then they also know the boat.

'We weren't followed. I'm sure of it but just keep an eye and you know where *it* is, if you need it.'

'I don't use guns, not if I can get away with it.'

I look at her, place my hand upon her cheek. 'And neither do I, but you know where *it* is.' And with that, I step out onto the Craigantlet deck before jumping into the tender with Susan.

'Do you think they'll come for her?' asks Susan.

Looking out on the water at Portree harbour, the daylight having left a twilight in the early hours of the morning, it will only be another couple of hours before the sun rises. I see the odd light on a boat but everything's calm and still. 'I don't know because I don't really know what's going on. But in the morning, we're having a good chat with her to find out what's really going on. And as for you, straight back, hotel room, bed, lock the door, keep your wits about you—anything suspicious, phone me.' Susan looks at me, her eyes opening wide. 'I don't know if it's this serious, Susan, but you treat it as such. Watch your back.'

Chapter Nine

I'm on the deck of Craigantlet looking across Portree Harbour. The sun's up, it's like full daylight, but it's only half past four in the morning. I haven't slept and I'm fortunate enough that Maggie's come up to keep me company here through most of the night. The air is cool for this time of year but I'm saying that it's not cold. I'm sitting in my jeans and t-shirt on deck, trying to think through what's going on. Something's afoot and I'm uneasy about what's happening.

Maggie can sense it, something bugging me and what I am feeling, even if she doesn't have much of an idea about the case itself. 'If something in your gut says it's wrong, it's probably wrong,' she says, 'and you need to keep an eye on who this is down below.'

'I wouldn't have seen it coming,' I say in a hushed tone, just in case our guest is awake. 'I wouldn't have reckoned that she was the pawn in this when she was there at the pools dancing. I could have sworn she was the one in charge, but then she could always just be the one passing out the information for someone else.'

'You did say she'd gone the previous night to her other house. You need to get a name for him, find out who he is, what he's doing; maybe he's at the centre of it.'

I take Maggie's hand, wrap it around me, placed my hand on top of hers and lean back into her. She pulls me close. 'But I need to read her,' I say. 'It's not serious yet.'

'Not serious yet? Somebody just tried to kill that woman,' says Maggie.

'So it would seem,' I say, but my voice is distant.

'You don't think they were faking it. It seems pretty close, all things considered; you don't set fire to a car with yourself inside, hoping to be rescued.'

'No, you don't, unless you know you can be rescued.'

'What do you mean?' says Maggie. 'She's been out cold.'

'But from when?' I say.

'From when?' says Maggie. 'Well, surely from when those men took her.'

'No, you said she was sedated; you said it seemed like sedation and if that's the case, when was she sedated? Was she self-sedated?'

I can feel Maggie lean off me, almost in frustration, as if I'm saying something stupid before she leans back in and quietly whispers in my ear, 'When was she doing that? She was in a car about to go off a cliff.'

'And that's a car I shouldn't have reached,' I say. 'When I started that run, I wasn't making it. But then the car somehow slows down, in the heat of the moment. I thought, oh, it's going uphill or something, but there was nothing for it to catch on, Maggie. Something slowed that car down.'

'What, do you think the men were watching, had some sort of remote control in the car? Well, sounds a bit high tech to me and you'll never know anyway, because the car's in the sea.'

'And it all sounds a bit James Bond too, nothing so overstaffed and nothing so clever. If she was awake, she'd know I'm coming, she'd slow the car down, ultimately, she can just put the brake on and stop and I can turn up and she'll say, "Oh, I just came round".

'Or she may have been sedated and you got lucky,' says Maggie. Maggie's right, it may have happened like that. Something's up here, something I don't like, so I'm going to tread very cautiously.

We hear a noise down in the cabin and Maggie goes down to see to our guest. When I descend into the main cabin and put the kettle on, I hear Maggie offering her some clothing before coming back out of the bunk room and telling me that she'd like a cup of tea as well. It's only a few seconds later that the cabin door opens and out walks Jenny Carnegie. She's got one of Maggie's t-shirts on, that stops around her hips but other than that she's simply in her underwear. I can see Maggie's eyes, angry, and I'm left wondering why Maggie simply would give her a t-shirt and not a lot more, but then, of course, she didn't. I reckon Jenny's overplaying this. But I feel an arm sneak around me, Maggie's, like she's claiming territory and I'm fine with that. But she's no need to do it—this territory is claimed.

I pour the tea and take it over to Jenny, telling her to sip it slowly. She takes the cup, her hands trembling and thanks me.

'You can finish dressing,' says Maggie. 'I left you some jeans in there.'

'I'm not sure they fit,' says Jenny; 'besides, I'm fine like this,' as she crosses over the bare legs, making sure I have a good view of them.

'I think you'll be fine in those jeans; your hips don't seem as big as Maggie's.'

I can feel the fire coming from Maggie but it is true that

Jenny has got much smaller hips and it's also my ploy to get her inside and wearing the jeans, which I thought Maggie would like. But I should have known better than to comment on a woman's shape and size in any fashion. Jenny looks up and I can see reluctance, but there's no way to get out of this as she walks back into the cabin, treks into the bunk room, and shuts the door. And with that Maggie turns to me, and mouths the word, 'hips'. I step forward, reach out, sneak my arm around her hips and pull her towards me. 'Yeah,' I whisper in her ear, 'proper hips.'

'Courtesy of Kirsten and Susan,' she says, 'but what on earth is she doing showing legs like that?'

'Like I said,' I whisper, 'I'm not convinced here.'

Jenny comes back out, wearing the jeans, and sits back in the original seat, again lifting up her leg. I feel an arm around me again and the two of us stand, looking at Jenny as she sips her tea. Her face is certainly bruised and from what Maggie told me, she has some bruising on her legs and in her upper torso as well but there's nothing broken. Nothing requiring a trip anywhere to get fixed.

'So, what's the deal, Mrs. Carnegie?'

She looks up, brushes her hair back and says, 'What's the deal with you? Maggie here says your name is Paddy, but that's all she says; who are you?' She begins to shake and her tea spills over the side. I don't like a messy cabin but I say nothing watching her, trying to see if this is put on or not.

'Your husband was worried about you, more worried you might be disappearing off to play with other men, which it turns out is true. Feel free to tell me about it, because those men seemed to want you dead last night.'

'It's not my fault; it's his fault, in a lot of ways. I was with him when he took me to the McAvoy's—that's where I met James McAvoy; that's where he came on to me. He said he had things on my husband, files and things, so I had to do what he said. He made me join this Druid Society, made me dance about. I didn't think anything of it. I just had to tell people things. There was nothing wrong. I dressed up, but it was nothing like religious or offensive and they watched as I danced. I don't mind being watched,' she says, smiling. 'Apparently, I have still got a figure that people—men—want to watch.'

With that, she leans back, pulling her shoulder blades back, making sure I can see the curves. I feel Maggie's arms tied around my waist. I put my arm around her. Why, when I am conducting an interview, does it feel like I'm being fought over?

'Why did he want you to do that?' I say. 'Why does he want you to dance and tell people things? What sort of things?'

'Surnames, places, that's all,' she says. 'I don't know any of them, I don't get it. But there's times, there's places, surnames I have to learn off and get rid of the paper. I tell them once, and that's it. And then you showed up this afternoon, both of you and then they come and they attack me. They must have seen you; did they come here? Do they know I'm here?' she says. The tea is shaking again.

'No, they don't know you're here,' I say, but I don't dissuade her of the idea that we were seen at the beach with her. I don't think we were but I think it's good that she says that.

'So how long has this bribery been going on? How long have you been with the druids?'

'It's coming up to a year and a half now,' she says. 'At first, my husband didn't notice but slowly, he's begun to.'

'And is that what they want from you, just to simply to dance about?'

'That's all they have wanted, nothing else,' she says, trying to look as innocent as possible.

'Well, you need to rest up,' I say. 'Why don't you go back into the bunk room and lie down.'

'What are you going to do?' she asks.

'Well, you tell me. Mr. McAvoy got you into this. I think it's only fair I go and find out how he's involved. In the meantime, if they think you're dead, you should stay here on the boat but stay down below. Maggie will stay up on top and keep a look out; if anyone's coming towards the boat, she's well capable of getting this thing moving.' I watch Jenny Carnegie stand up and make her way into my bunk room. Once she shuts the door, I make my way over to a false section at the side of the boat, open it, pull out a small handgun, and give it to Maggie. It's not the largest weapon but it will fit inside a pocket. I've seen Maggie handle a gun before; she knows what she's doing, but she takes it very solemnly when I hand her the weapon.

'You think she's that much of a risk?' she whispers to me.

'I really don't know but you are here with her, so if needs be, use it. I need to find out what's happening. I'd like to bring Susan here with you, then at least there would be two of you with her, but Susan's running cover.'

'Why don't you bring Martha?' says Maggie. 'She seems to know how to operate well; she looked after us last time.'

'That's a good idea,' I say. 'Let's see if I can get hold of her, but in the meantime, you stay up on deck, she stays below, and you don't leave anywhere without that weapon.'

Maggie nods and disappears up onto the deck while I start to busy myself getting ready to head across. It's still early in the morning, so I might be able to get out and see the man in his home, see if I can find anything out about him. As I reach around for my jacket and other bits and pieces, the door of the bunk room opens and out steps Jenny Carnegie, I turn around and see her bare legs, the jeans have been removed again.

'I think you should go and sleep. I'm just disappearing off,' I say and turn my back to her. I'd like to say that I didn't enjoy the view. I'd like to say that it was no problem looking away but I had to hand it to her: for her age, she has an incredible figure and clearly, she works on it. But I get the feeling it's like a marksman works on his weapon making sure the rifle can shoot. Marksmen will clean and polish every bit of it, strip it down to build it back up again and I get the feeling that's how Jenny sees her body. Her arm snakes around me and I feel her pull up close to me.

'Now you're in my life, Paddy,' she says. 'Are you sure there isn't anything I can do for you? Why don't you send her off? Go and get some groceries, that could give us an hour or two.' Her hands stroke my chest and as they move further down, I grab one, taking it off, holding it clear of me. I turn to her face, putting mine up against hers.

'I think you need to understand something. You are actually in my care; your husband employed me, so he's my client—you're my client's wife. One thing I do not do is jump into bed with a client's wife. Secondly, you owe me nothing. I don't know who you are yet; I don't know if you're telling the truth. All I know is what you've told me. You may be covering this up. You may have been cheating on him the whole time. My duty is to my client. So kindly stay here, put your jeans on and go and lie down in the bunk room. The woman upstairs will look after you if you need it.'

She looks rebuked, turns around, and walks away but she moves those small hips up and down and I noticed that her underwear, her pants, are halfway down her backside which she's jiggling. She stops at the door, turns around, leaning towards me. 'If you're sure, but the offer's always there.'

'I prefer bigger hips,' I say. Then I see Jenny Carnegie looking up to the hatch, before quickly disappearing inside the bunk room, the door closing behind her.

'Good choice of words,' says Maggie and climbs down inside the cabin. She comes over and wraps her arms around me and whispers in my ear, 'Cheeky girl, she better understands who owns this.'

'She might not, but as I said before, just watch your back, keep an eye. I'll be back soon enough, with Martha or Susan.' And with that, I step out onto the deck, jump into the tender, and head off to the harbour side looking to hail a taxi to pick up my car from the previous night.

Chapter Ten

I'm not keen on leaving Maggie, but if I stay and simply watch our new guest on Craigantlet, it will be very obvious I suspect her, and at the moment, I want her to think I'm simply investigating what her husband thinks is wrong with their marriage. One of the things that you find doing this work is you get a very suspicious mind and you can end up thinking the worst of everyone. Unfortunately, sometimes the worst is true, but try and tell that to other people you've offended on the way when it hasn't been.

After picking up my own car, I drive off to see James McAvoy, plunking myself just a little way away from his house. It's still early in the morning and my stomach says I should have grabbed something more substantial to eat before starting out. The day is bright and I realize just how picturesque a setting his house is in. Fields roll around it and behind it—it's just a tapestry of large hills, perfect for climbing and walking around. The small farm around his holdings with a small number of cattle also adds to the picture postcard.

Around seven o'clock, he comes out to see to his cattle before returning to his doorstep, or rather his wife standing, waiting for him, in what looks like a rather warm dressing gown. There's no gentle kiss or embrace; instead, she's questioning him about something that she seems agitated about, moving back and forward to his car while she harasses him with more questions. Look, maybe she's justified, but it seems to me she's going about this the wrong way. The man's getting upset, very upset and I can see the clenching of fists. She comes after him again and all of a sudden, he turns with a swing of the arm, striking her across the face with the back of his hand. She's barely left standing and goes to run off, but he grabs her, holding her by the dressing gown, forcing her to kiss him. There's venom in her eyes, but she looks stuck, not strong enough to force him off.

A child comes to the door and she turns her head, mouthing something like 'Mommy will be in soon,' smiling, before turning back, to produce that face of venom again.

They both disappear inside and about an hour later Mr. McAvoy comes to the door; his wife comes out to watch him depart, but now dressed in jeans and a jumper. I can feel the heat of the day already begin, as I see him open his boot and throw in a briefcase, he then shuts the boot and turns back calling the woman over. Again, her face is like thunder, but she walks over obediently and he takes her in his arms briefly, enjoys her for a moment before sending her back to the house, with a smack on her backside. It makes me feel pretty sick, to be honest, watching it, because I can tell a coerced woman when I see one. She looks like the pleasant type too.

When he departs the house, McAvoy takes the main road down to Portree, stopping by what looks like a small hotel. I see him go to the boot, delve inside for it, possibly opening his briefcase and holding an envelope. He takes it and walks into the hotel and I make my way up to the door, to see him hand it to a man inside. I don't go in, lingering at the door, pretending

I'm looking for someone, just casting my eye in through the glass-fronted panes.

The man receiving the letter looks angry and gives a shout to McAvoy, waving him away with a hand, as if he should just disappear. McAvoy looks around him and without seeing anyone, reaches forward and grabs the man by the collar. It's only for a moment; when McAvoy just walks away, I can see the fear in the man's eyes.

Stepping back from the glass door, I let McAvoy walk past me and watch him rifle into his boot again, taking out another letter before walking off down one of the main streets. I follow and find myself at a hostel. He steps inside, forcing me to remain close behind. I pretend that I am a guest by walking past him and on through to the gents' toilets. Once in there, I'm able to open the door slightly and look out.

This stunning young woman, possibly mid-twenties arrives, but as soon she's sees who it is, her face becomes strained. She's in a pair of shorts and a t-shirt and given the weather that's about to build up outside, that seems pretty reasonable. I can hear some of her words and she's also standing a distance from the man, clearly afraid of him. He steps forward, forcing her back towards the corner of the room. There are doors out on either side, but this doesn't seem to bother him as he steps forward, looming over from close range.

She takes the letter and reads it before throwing it on the floor, swearing, but his hand shoots out, grabbing her by the cheek. I catch the words 'be a good girl' before seeing him stand there, his eyes roaming up and down her, like she's a piece of meat. It obviously makes her sick to her core, but she doesn't turn away; there's obviously something holding her there, some reason she can't move. He has her in his grasp, whether it's coercion or money or whatever. I'm really beginning to dislike this man.

He leaves after complimenting her on her top, but not in a nice way. As he walks out the door, I see her bend over and begin to cry. Stepping out from behind the toilet door, I see her shocked face. I smile politely, apologizing and tell her I got caught short and didn't know where to go. I offer to pay for the use of the toilets, but she's too choked up, still crying. I feign an innocence, wondering what's wrong with her.

'Are you all right?' I ask. 'Is there something I can do to help?'

The woman sniffs back some tears, 'No it's okay, just bad news.'

'Sorry, I couldn't help it, I was just about to come out of the door and I saw him. It really wasn't pleasant what he was doing there.' She looks with horror at me. 'I mean he was just staring at you, sizing you up.'

'No, it wasn't nice,' she says and turns away. 'Don't worry about the toilets—it's fine.' And with that she moves her hand to dismiss me, but I decide to chance my arm further.

'Are you sure you're okay, nothing I can help with? Do you need me to get the police?'

At this, she spins round, her face almost angry. 'No, I don't need the police. I don't need your help; now please just go,' she says. I take the hint and walk out of the door, but inside, I feel quite cold about what I'd seen. The woman's quite young and has obviously started up this business and they are taking it from her or at least making her pay through the nose for it. Now that's bad enough but I guess the criminal fraternity will just turn around and say 'it's business.' The way in which he was working her, emotionally, sexually, really disgusted me and inside something tells me that I'm going to bring this guy down whatever happens.

Outside in the street, I tail back to realize his car is still where he parked it. I sit and watch it for another twenty minutes before he returns and drives off. It's to the other side of the town we go, to a range of chalets with a rather quaint kids' play area. Once again, he digs into his boot before heading over to what looks like the main administration building. I have to watch him from a distance this time, as the terrain doesn't offer me the chance to get close and there's not enough people to hide amongst. This time it's a middle-aged woman coming to the door and I see him once again hand over a letter, which causes some great distress. The blonde-haired woman rises up in her heels, pulls back her shoulder and throws the letter back at him. I see his hand begin to rise but she's telling him something. As if nothing matters, she then spits in his face.

In all his dealings so far, he's been cool and calm, but at this point, his hand goes out, grabs her by the jugular and pushes her back through the door behind her, inside the administration building. The door slams shut, and I run over to find out what's going on.

'You'll do as you're told, bitch,' comes a voice from inside and I can hear a couple of hard slaps to someone's face. There's a part of me that instinctively wants to run in and floor the guy but I'm also working undercover and if I blow it now, I could end up not seeing what's really going on. So, as much as it sickens me, the woman has to endure another couple of slaps to the face while I wait outside.

'You won't get any more of my money, now piss off,' she yells at him, and I think I hear her spit again. This time there's a proper commotion and I watch him grab her, holding her by the hair and pushing her face first, towards the wall. He's got her held tight and she's obviously in some distress. He's up close to the side of her face and I can't hear what he's saying; I'm hoping it's merely a reminder to pay her money, but he seems to have a mood on him as he continues to hold her head against the wall. He steps back half a pace and looks up and down. I really don't like the way this is going.

'You'll do as you're told and because of your cheek, I think I need an extra payment.' With that, I see him start to unbuckle his belt. There are times when you see things hit a limit. When I'm in the shadows watching, sometimes I have to see good people get roughed up. It's not ideal and hopefully I get things turned around in the end, but I really don't want to have to sit and watch. That being said, as long as things don't go too out of hand, I can handle it but this is getting out of hand very quickly. I can't abide this sort of thing and the moment he reaches down, grabbing the woman's skirt and pulling it up over her buttocks, I can't stand outside anymore.

I throw open the door, march in, and say, 'Is this the booking office?' and then hold my words, looking at the sight, waiting for the man to back down, but he doesn't.

'Get the hell out, son,' he shouts at me. 'Get out, you one-armed freak, before I put you up against the wall and do you as well!'

I had hoped he would simply back down, say something about him being caught and just having a bit of fun but his response sets me on edge. And as for the comment about me being a one-armed freak, well, let's just say I'm now going to enjoy what I'm about to do.

'Leave the woman alone,' I say. She's crying, there's panic shuttering through her body, and I wonder has he ever done this before? Or has he simply gone up a level? I would say the

84

latter.

As I step forward, he keeps one arm on her head, but turns to face me, 'I said get the hell out!' he spits, 'or I'll rip the other arm off as well.'

The element of surprise when taking somebody on a combat is always what you want and I lumber forward like any sort of Tom, Dick, or Harry who was just passing. Since losing the arm, I've trained in martial arts. I use my feet a lot more than I used to and I'm a lot nimbler than I ever thought possible. Stepping forward, I see him let her head go, coming at me with both fists raised.

He swings one and I lean back out of the way, as the other fist comes in. I swing back from that as well, but now he's totally off balance having missed on both accounts. Making sure my left leg is planted, I strike straight up with my right, catching him on the chin and the guy collapses to the ground.

'What sort of a freak are you?' he shouts, getting back to his feet and charging at me. I sidestep, leave a foot out, causing him to trip and go headlong. He's really just a big thug and he certainly doesn't know how to fight but he gets up one more time, I guess out of wounded pride at being beaten apart by an amputee. This time he comes at me with both arms. I sidestep, throw my arm around the neck, pulling it tight as his feet scramble along with his hands to get punches on any part of me. But I kick hard into the back of his knees and he drops to them.

'Get out,' I say. 'If I see you here again, with any hands on this woman then next time I won't let you walk out.' I release my grip, step away a couple of paces lest he comes after me again. I stand between him and the woman. He stares at me, looking grim, before walking out the door.

I can hear the woman crying behind me, but they're tears of relief. Of course, she's traumatized; of course, she's upset, but she has just been saved from an awful fate. Once I've made sure he's disappeared, I turn back to her and realize she still has her face in her hands, her skirt still up above her backside. I gently step forward and give it a pull down, regaining her modesty.

'You okay, love? I chased him off, but do you want me to get the police?'

She shakes her head. 'No, it's okay. Thank you.'

'Is he liable to come back?' I ask.

'It's okay.' she says.

'I don't mean to be funny, love, but do you have a man over here?'

She nods, 'My husband, he's in the hospital, he should be out in a day.'

'In the hospital? What's up with him?' I ask.

'He was attacked the other night,' and she says no more. I think I understand why.

'I really think you should call in the police.'

'I did,' she says, 'but he's involved with them.'

'Who?' I ask.

'The policemen who came with him when he came round.'

'Look, I might've chased him away for a couple of days at least, but if you need me, please call.'

I hand her my card and she looks down at it. 'Private investigator?' she says.

'Yes,' I say. 'I can tell he's extorting you and I'm looking into it. Keep that card quiet but if you get any more trouble, ring my number and I'll come and help.' She looks at me, gives a faint smile. 'Okay, but I doubt you can do anything,' and with that, she starts crying again. I step forward, allowing her to lean on my shoulder and take her to a seat. I look around and see a kettle in the room next door. I leave her for a minute, while I make a cup for her. When I come back, she takes it and sips it. The tears are still flowing.

'He was really going to do that, wasn't he?' she says. 'Really going to . . .' Her voice stops.

'Yes, he was,' I say in a very matter of fact statement. 'You have my number and I can sort things out. If money is an issue, it isn't. Call me if you need me.'

I watch her nod her head. I check with her once more if she's okay before I leave but it's one of those situations because in the long run, she probably isn't going to be okay. But for now, she's at least safe.

Stepping outside, I realize that I've lost my tail, that he's disappeared off somewhere. So, I give Susan a call. She's still in her hotel but I tell her I'll meet her there very shortly because I might change up the job that she's on. It's one thing to threaten people but this guy seemed to enjoy what he was doing and certainly with the women he wanted to take it to a different level. Everything just got a whole lot darker.

Chapter Eleven

When I arrive at Susan's hotel, she's at the door and runs over to meet me. I can understand this because she's been working a lot on her own and it does get lonely, so to see a friendly face always causes a little bit of excitement. But as she approaches, my mind thinks back to the woman who I saw being attacked and the thought that if Susan gets in the way of these people, they might try and do that to her. For a man of that ilk, someone like Susan—young, red hair, and growing into the prime of her life—might be too much of a temptation. The days when I worked alone were much easier, but I won't let this affect my smiling face as we sit down to get a spot of lunch. It's only a bowl of soup each, but wiht no one about the menu is limited. It's quite obvious what Susan says about the hotel having no guests and we're the only ones in their dining room.

The soup is quite good and I wait until the owner disappears back out of the room before I update Susan on what happened today. I give her a serious talk about the dangers that she could face if she gets too closely involved in this. I'm reminded that if she thinks she's in trouble or someone's coming after her, she gets out as fast as she can. I check she has a contact button with her, an alarm she can set off which gives GPS tracking.

After the previous episode on Mull, Hans advised it. It's like one of those beacons they use to track down people lost in the mountains, or on a boat but it's smaller, very discreet and hangs around her neck in the shape of a small cross; it looks like a piece of jewellery and so if she's trapped, nervous, she can easily fumble it, setting it off without arousing suspicion. I have to hand it to Hans—it's one of his best devices yet.

Once the soup's done, we order some coffee. I tell Susan that I want her to start following James McAvoy but from a distance. She needs to make a note of the places he goes to, but under no circumstances is she to tail him inside any of them. I reiterate what happened to me and while I stepped in when necessary because things were getting out of hand, I don't want her to be doing that. God knows if he overcame her, subdued her, she'd get that fate. I'm usually quite light when I talk to Susan, but this is very intense, extremely serious, so I make my point and I hope she takes it.

I get a call from Martha telling me she's going to be on Skye by evening and she'll make her way out to Portree harbour. I tell her to ring me when she gets there, and I'll get her across on the tender. She says she's been looking into things and, in a way that only Martha can, she advises that she's looked into Skye accommodations and been able to isolate a large number of businesses on the island who seem to be struggling in the height of the tourist season. There're complaints that there aren't enough spaces, and yet people aren't booking up certain hotels or guest houses. She's trying to find out why but that's obviously a lot more difficult than simply breaking in to find out booking numbers.

I tell Susan that I can really do with a shower and does she mind if I borrow the one in her room. There are places up and around where Craigantlet is moored, but I set off so early this morning, I'm not even sure they were open. She nods and leads me up to her room. I lock the door behind me before jumping in for a quick shower, dry myself, and changing back into my clothes, exit the bathroom. I find her lying on the bed, examining what Martha sent to me.

'This could be quite extensive, Paddy,' she says. 'The number of hotels and stuff. I reckon there's at least thirty businesses here.'

'I agree, and if those are the ones that don't have people in them and are being extorted, all those other ones do have people in them that are paying their money to these people. It would take more than one man to carry this all out.' We check out of the room, make our way back down out into the car park, where I notice that whereas there were three cars when I came in, there now seems to be at least six. But with these six cars, there's no activity, there's no more people about. I tell Susan to come over to the car with me and we sit inside.

After five minutes, she says,' Paddy, what are we doing? Why are we just sitting here watching?'

'Just a hunch,' I say. 'Double the number of cars in the car park, no more people moving about. We said we were the only people here, nobody else is staying at the hotel, so how come these cars are here? Something's going on.'

It takes another ten minutes before I see what's happening. A number of young men walk into the car park with hoodies up and masks pulled up over their faces. The boot of the car is open, and I see them with baseball bats now stepping towards the hotel and I count possibly twelve making their way straight through the front door.

'Susan, stay here, call the police,' I say.

'Where are you going?' she says. 'You can't take on twelve of them.'

'No, but I might be able to get him clear before he gets a bloody beating.' And with that I scarper off, but not to the front door, instead searching for the rear. I find the kitchen entrance at the back of the building and bursting in, see a woman cooking.

'Where's your owner?'

'He through to the front. Why?'

'Get out! Get out! Go to the car park. There's a girl in a car there, get into that car!'

'Why, what's going on?'

'Somebody has come to do your boss in.' I see her look at me and realize what she's thinking. 'Not me, there's some young ones come in to beat him up; I'm going to save him. Get out to the car, now!' I yell this at her before running through the door that leads to the restaurant. I see one of the hoodlums and he clocks me from the far end. The owner's also at the other end and as he looks up, I see the fear in his eyes.

'He's in here, and the freak as well. The freak's only got one arm—we'll do him easy.' The young man runs forward with a baseball bat, straight towards me. Since he said the word freak which you may by now be realizing annoys me, I decide I am not holding back on him. As he approaches to swing the bat, I step forward into him, which he isn't expecting, planting my fist right onto his jaw. This forward momentum takes the feet right from under him while my fist drives his head back and he falls to the floor. But I don't want to stay where I am.

The owner is behind me, and he's in the corner of the room. If I can get between some tables, I might be able to cut down the number of them that can come at us at once. I don't know if the guy can fight, he looks in his sixties. He certainly wouldn't be up for much.

As I turn and run to them, putting myself between the man and the approaching thugs, I realize that this could be painful. Hopefully, Susan will get the police here quickly. The first thug steps forward, swinging a bat. I lean back to avoid it and step forward driving a knee up into his groin. As he howls at that, my fist drives at his face, giving him a bloody nose as he falls backwards. But then another one comes forward swinging a bat. This catches me in the side.

They say you've got to roll with the punches but when the punch comes from a baseball bat, it's not that easy and another one reigns down on my shoulder. I'm able to drive forward getting close to them, so they can't swing the bats. It's not my preferred style, I prefer to have someone come on to me and take them out with my legs, but a bat effectively puts paid to that type of defence.

So now I am close and start driving knees up and into them. I'm stuck between two tables so only two of them are coming at me at once and I drive knees up into them. They howl in pain as I put myself upright and then headbutt one, right on the nose breaking it. But there's no time to stop as I feel a punch catch me in the side of the head. With my hand up, grabbing the guy's nose, driving my fingers up as hard as I can, he moves back shouting, but another two step forward, baseball bats swinging. I manage to slip to one side as the bat crashes onto the table but the other player catches me with a punch to the face and I feel blood come from my nose.

One slips past me and he starts to beat the owner across the head. Dodging my own assailant, I then drive this guy into the wall where his head ricochets off of a lamp shade. He collapses to the ground, and I drive a kick into his face. I'm in a situation with so many that I can't hold back, I can't just simply try and arrest them. This is more like survival because if I take a blow to the head, it could be the last one. That's the trouble with blunt instruments, people think they're for beating people up, but they can kill just as easily.

The pressure starts to become too much and I feel someone grab my arm. My back is forced down and I shout out loud, swearing, as I catch him with a kick to the side. But there's too many of them and they're over the top of me and I think this could really be trouble.

The shot reverberates around the inside of the restaurant and all of a sudden, I'm left lying there, a prone proprietor beside me. As the thugs take off, I pull myself to my feet looking at the far end of the restaurant. It won't be a policeman; they don't carry guns here. Instead, I see the red hair of my partner's daughter and a smiling face.

'Get that gun away before the police get here. I don't know how we're going to explain a gunshot in the ceiling.'

'It's only blanks, Paddy, only blanks.'

'Nonetheless, get it away before they get here.' With that she disappears outside before running back in and coming over to me to ask if I'm all right. I shake my head but indicate she should check the proprietor first. I can hear the sirens now and in another couple of minutes, the officers come running inside, to see two of us sitting on the floor and Susan attending to the head wound of the hotel owner.

It took about an hour before I was ready to leave. I was checked over by an ambulance crew and they said I had quite bad bruising, but nothing else seemed to be out of place. I certainly didn't have a concussion, unlike the proprietor who was pretty senseless by the end of it. Susan patched him up the best she could, but the ambulance guys really knew what they were doing, and he disappeared off in the back of it. The police constable who took my statement advised me that this was not uncommon at the moment. I was, in fact the eighth beating in recent weeks.

'Can I just ask?' I say. 'Were they all against hospitality establishments? People providing accommodation?'

He looks at me before consulting his colleague. 'Yeah, we think so. I think they all were. Why do you ask that?'

I pull out my card and hand it to him and I see a face that doesn't really approve. 'Well, keep yourself safe, sir; they're a nasty piece of work, this lot.'

'You don't have to tell me. Do you have any idea why they're doing this though?'

'It's a matter under investigation,' he says, 'but it looks like a lot of young hoods. Who knows how they get their kicks.'

'They may be a lot of young hoodlums but they park three cars out there with all the gear in the back of it to do the damage. That's planning, proper planning. It doesn't sound just like a load of thugs to me.'

The man raises his eyebrows, becomes very noncommittal but he asks that if I find anything out, I let him know, and gives me the card for the station. If I find anything out, I think to myself, and I can nail the bastards, you're darn right you'll get a phone call. But at the moment I still don't know what's going on. Who is the woman on the boat and what's she doing?

Once we're cleared to leave, I tell Susan to go stake out the McAvoy's and I'll be in touch. As for me, I'm heading back to the boat. I want to see how this woman plays it when I report what has happened. And also, I want a little bit of TLC from

Maggie because these bruises are smarting like anything.

Chapter Twelve

'Stay still,' says Maggie, as she dabs some more ointment on the bruises across my back. I rear at her touching, but a soothing hand goes across my neck as well, easing me down. I'm sitting with my shirt off in the main cabin of Craigantlet, Maggie working away at my back while I'm being watched by Jenny Carnegie. She's giving me eyes that say, 'That looks painful', and it's like she's trying to sympathize, but I'm not buying it. But I smile when she looks across trying to feign some sort of camaraderie and thanks.

'So, it's just kids then,' she says. 'These kids just came round and beat him up; it seems a bit extreme that they're running these things.'

'It was definitely kids—maybe nineteen to twenty—but why beat up a hotel owner here? It's also empty and there's really little to gain from it for them.'

'Did you get to look at any of them?' asks Maggie.

'No, they were all masked, I couldn't see faces. The owner's gone to the hospital as well, but I don't think he's going to talk; something was scaring him, scaring him bad.'

'Maybe you could try McAvoy again,' says Jenny Carnegie. 'I know what he did to me; maybe he's involved. What'd you think?'

'I haven't got a lot of links for that,' I say. 'I really could do with finding out about these hoodlums and what's going on there.'

'Well, I've got someone I know in the police,' says Jenny. 'Maybe you could talk to him, share what you know with him.'

'How do you know him?' I ask.

'Used to be an old flame.'

'Did you not go about all the stuff has been happening to you?'

She shakes her head, 'No, I was too scared but you could put it to him; you could talk about McAvoy with him, keep my name out of it in case anything comes back to McAvoy. What do you think?' she says. She leans over towards me, showing some cleavage and I can feel Maggie's press on my back getting that little bit stronger. The woman tries to use every charm she's got to wangle me into the path she wants me to go. I reckon it's a path I want to follow to find out what she's really playing at, but Maggie's not going to take well to it.

'Give me his name and his number and I'll get in contact,' I say and sure enough, there's a press on my back of ointment that's a lot stronger than it should be.

'Are you done yet, Maggie?' I say, and then comes another hard press on my back. 'I need to get changed. You probably could as well.'

Maggie's stressed as it is and unlike me who's been involved in a bit of a scuffle, she looks fine. But I can sense her wondering why I'm telling her she should be getting dressed. I look up at Jenny and say, 'If you can give us a moment?' before taking Maggie's hand and leading her through to the bunk room. I shut the door behind me, but I know it's no serious filter to conversation.

I turn to face Maggie and see she has an annoyed face on her. I reach forward with my arm and pull her close, giving her a kiss on the lips before moving my head to the side and whispering in her ear, 'Just pretend we're having a cuddle or something. I need to talk to you on the quiet.'

'What the hell are you doing? She's throwing herself at you,' she whispers in my ear.

'Leaning forward like that, letting everyone have a good view.'

'Calm down. I know fine rightly what she's doing and that's why I'm going to see her policeman. I want to know who it is. I've got my own policeman, so don't worry. I'm also going to go and see McAvoy and see what he's up to because I don't think he's what we think he is.

'You need to stay here,' I continue, 'and keep an eye on her. I don't want her running about yet until I can get a handle on what's going on. Once I do, I'll let her go, find out what's happening. You able to do that?'

She pulls me closer, whispering in my ear, 'Of course, just take care and tell Susan to take care too. I don't trust this woman.'

With that we break off and I put on a change of clothes, grabbing my jeans and a shirt. I turn to see Maggie changing. With the warm weather, she's putting on a pair of shorts and a top that hugs her. It's very alluring and enjoyable, but I reach over and whisper to her, 'You don't have to compete.'

She replies to this, 'Can I not look good for my man?' I give her a kiss, pull her close and tell her how wonderful she looks before walking out of the cabin.

I go through to the main cabin and see Jenny, legs crossed, in her pair of shorts and leaning back with her blouse half open.

'Have you got that number for me?' I ask, to which she hands me a piece of paper. The pad says Sergeant Gillespie and gives a number and I thank Jenny for it. I tell her I'll be back later in the day and tell her if she needs anything to tell Maggie who can ring me. I climb outside onto the deck with Maggie following, and as I'm about to get into the tender, she reaches over and touches my shoulder.

'Careful this time,' she says, 'some of those bruises are bad. If you had taken the bat to the head . . .'

'I know, but if I hadn't stepped in, he'd have been a lot worse.'

'And be careful with the police guy; if he's working with her, you don't know what you're going to get.'

I nod. 'But on the other hand, they want to know what I know at the moment and that's going to be fed very slowly.' I hug her, kiss her, and then leave on the tender, noting she watches me all the way across the harbour.

It's tough for Maggie. She's babysitting a woman, who frankly seems to engage with men in any way. Trying to use her flesh to attract us but who's playing a very dangerous game. I'm sure she's in the middle of it and that means she's dangerous and a lot of me is trusting that Maggie's streetwise enough, but she seems to be.

Martha should be here soon and when she is, it will put my mind more at ease. If you looked at Maggie and Martha, you'd think that Maggie was the one more capable. She's in good shape for her years—physically capable and mentally quite sharp as well. But Martha's used to dealing with nasty people although when you look at her, you think she's extremely overweight. But she has a sharp mind and she's one step ahead of the game and despite not looking physically fit, she can handle herself. Because when she hits, she hits to the right place. Yes, I'll feel more comfortable when Martha's here.

Once I get to land, tie up the tender, and take my car, I make a phone call to Susan. I tell her to make sure she's staying safe when looking out for Mr. McAvoy, to find out what he's doing from a distance, not to get close and not to engage. The main reason for this is that I want to get to find out what he's doing. I don't want them interrupted thinking somebody is on to him.

When I speak to Susan, she's quite anxious. Like Maggie, she's worried about the beating that went on, but I tell her to keep her distance. At the first sign of trouble, just drive away and get in touch and I tell her if she gets pursued at all, she's just to drive right back down to Stranraer. If necessary, walk into a police station. The last thing I need is Susan getting grabbed, like happened to us last time. I know she knows it's one of the risks when she signed up to it, but I still don't want it to happen. And she's not streetwise enough yet to get herself back out quickly.

I make a phone call to Sergeant Gillespie, who seems incredibly keen to meet me. I tell him I got his number from Jenny Carnegie and there's almost no hesitation in asking me to meet. He suggests we meet towards the shore, quite far away, but I'm not up for that. I don't know this man from Adam. So, I tell him to meet me at a cafe in the middle of Portree. There'll be plenty of people about, and I've got no problem talking in low hushed tones. He's apparently off duty so he'll be there in half an hour.

The man is six feet five. I swear he had trouble getting in through the door of the cafe. And when he comes to my table, he looms over me like some sort of giant. His hands look like bats. When he brings a mug of coffee back and sits down in front of me, the coffee's in some sort of China teacup compared to those hands, yet when I look at mine, my hand barely gets around the cup at all. He's wearing dark jeans and one of those muscle type tops which emphasizes how impressive his pecs are. Part of me wonders if this is how Jenny Carnegie knows him. He's certainly not afraid to show off his body and as I know of her, she's not afraid to show off hers.

The man sits down opposite me, staring into my eyes and then simply says, 'So you're Patrick Smythe.'

'That's me. Does the lack of an arm give it away?' It seems to unnerve him, as it does many people, and generally that's why I use it. I like them to be uncomfortable. These days I'm more comfortable without my arm. Maybe that's not exactly true. People don't know how much I'd give to have my arm back but at the end of the day, it's happened to me and I've learned to live with it, whereas other people, even enemies just don't seem to want to talk about it.

'So why does Jenny want you to talk to me?' asks the man.

'You aware of her problems?' I say, raising my eyebrows.

'She had said, in the past, that some guys have troubled her.'

'Well, somebody tried to kill her, somebody from the group that goes out and dances round the Fairy Pools. I take it you're aware of them.'

'The druids?' he says, 'Oh, we're all aware of the druids, Jenny being daft enough to be part of it. I wouldn't mind seeing her dancing though.'

I put it on a profoundly serious face. 'You need to understand somebody tried to kill her. The group took her away, they put her in a car, tried to launch it off a cliff, and fortunately, I managed to save her.'

'What were you doing there?'

'I've been employed by her husband, to find out where she's going at the moment; he's been worried about her disappearing off. Apparently, he's not aware of her druidic commitments.'

The man looks at me and then nods, 'Jenny's always liked to play around; she likes a good-looking man.'

'I take it she's played around with you then. Don't blame you, she's a good-looking woman.'

'More than just good looking,' he says.

Just in case you're wondering, I'm not okay with this idea of playing around, but I need to buy into it with him, see what he gets from this arrangement. I could believe that he gets up close and personal access and she plays him like that. She's particularly good at it; drawing a guy in towards her.

'So, what do you know, Mr. Smythe, and where is Jenny at the moment?'

'Jenny's safe and she's safe of her own free will,' I say, 'but she said I should contact you about the beating up of a hotel proprietor that I was a witness to. In fact, I ended up defending him, taking some shocking blows from a group of hoods.'

'Ah, this I do know about,' he says. 'They've been going around, beating up several people. Not been looking good on the public image front.'

'Will you give out the names of the people that these hoods have been beating up?'

The man shakes his head. 'It's a police matter which you should keep out of, Mr. Smythe.'

'Okay,' I say, knowing that I can get Martha to dig in and find it anyway, 'but I'm going to go and have a look at James McAvoy—he seems to be acting very strangely.' As I see it, I need to feed something into this relationship or it's going to die quickly. 'He's been having problems with his wife by the looks of it, getting stressed. I also noticed that at the druid gatherings, people seem to be passing messages and there's something going on. As I understand it, Mr. McAvoy has certain properties as well as his farm, so I'll need to look into those.'

'Keep an eye on him and keep me informed of his movements,' says the man. 'By the sounds of it, he's worth keeping an eye on, but we've not got a uniform we could spare, and at the moment there's not much to go on. And keep her safe,' says the Sergeant. 'I go back a bit with Jenny; in fact if you want, if you show me where she's staying, I'll try and keep an eye on her as well.'

'It's fine.' There's no way I'm going to let this guy near Maggie. 'She's safe with some associates of mine, but she's free to go whenever she wants. But I'll certainly keep you in touch with what's happening with Mr. McAvoy. Do you think Jenny's sleeping around is getting her into trouble in the middle of something else?'

'Maybe she's seen something she shouldn't,' the man says, 'but I'm sure they'd be quite forgiving, certainly with Jenny's talents.'

I don't tell him about her other liaison, because I feel that that will get back to Jenny and I need to know who that man is. Martha's arrival should bring me some much-needed information.

Sergeant Gillespie leaves the coffee house before I get myself another cup and sit down to think. I need to make the connection between these beatings and what's being said at these druidic gatherings. Something's not right, but at the moment, Mr. McAvoy seems to be the main player in all this. He's obviously got something to do, something that Jenny needs him to do, and wants to make sure he's doing. I also haven't called her husband; he doesn't seem to be paying me a lot of attention, considering the fact that he's paying my wage and wondering if his wife's sleeping around. I kind of expected a little bit more contact. As I'm downing the last of my coffee, the mobile phone rings. It's Susan and she sounds quite agitated.

'Paddy, I've just been watching James McAvoy and he's had a bit of an accident.'

'Accident? 'I say, my heart sinking, wondering if something's happened to the man. 'What do you mean?'

'Well, he's just been moping around today, hanging out around and about his farm, but I've seen him drinking several times. He's had this flask and I'm sure he's gone back into the house to fill it once or twice. But he got on his quad bike, driving around on his farm and he smacked it into a wall. He's come off it, but he looks quite stunned. His wife came down and it looked like she wanted to take him to the hospital, but he's waved her off. I think he was telling her things to do, but I wasn't close enough to get words.'

'Good stuff,' I say to her. 'Just keep an eye on him and I'll be over soon. I think I need to have a word with Mr. McAvoy.'

Chapter Thirteen

I t's getting late now, heading towards the evening and I meet up with Susan, who is sitting watching McAvoy's house. As I the jump into the car, she leans over, gives me a hug and a little peck on the cheek. I can tell she's a little bit nervous, and seeing that beating earlier on the day, it's probably upset her. But she's been holding it together, keeping an eye on things for me, and wisely keeping her distance.

'How you feeling, Paddy?' she says.

'Well your mum's done wonders on it, but my back's still smarting. Don't get too close to a baseball bat like that.' I try to laugh but frankly it's actually a little sore if I do.

'I think he may have been sleeping off the last couple of hours,' says Susan, 'after his accident. But where have you been?'

I update Susan on the latest happenings and advise her it's important that she stays incognito, out of the way, but she's delighted to know I brought coffee. As we sit and drink, my mobile phone goes and it's Martha. She says she's about to get onto the tender and head out to Craigantlet which I know will be an experience for her. Martha hates small boats. I tell her to ring ahead and advise Maggie and I give Martha a lowdown on what's been happening.

She says she's also found out that our mystery lover of Jenny

Carnegie is a Simon Hilden, who's not only a landowner but also has a lot of accommodations on Skye, accommodations that seem to be doing rather well at this time—unlike Susan's hotel.

'As far as I can tell,' says Martha, 'he's fairly clean and there's not a lot I can tag on him, but he certainly has had a lot of competitors give up beside him. He's reasonably new in the Skye area, bought his house only two years ago, and I can't find anything to indicate that he's been long-term involved with Jenny Carnegie other than that. Everything I'm looking at for you indicates accommodations, places for people to stay, all different types. You also should be aware that the number of beatings in Skye has increased over the last while.'

'I was becoming aware of that. I was beat up myself today.'

There's a dip in her voice. 'Are you sure you're okay? Do you need any assistance? Should we get Hans in?'

She's—Martha—always the first to worry when things get rough, but it's understandable. She doesn't like that end of it, much happier behind the desk, working things out.

'I'm fine,' I say. 'Nothing that the ministrations of a good woman can't put right. Just be aware, the woman you're going to babysit is in the middle of this so she could be quite rough herself. Take precautions and keep an eye on Maggie for me.'

When I close the phone on Martha, I see movement in the house. The lights are on and I know the children are probably thinking about heading to bed but instead I see our man move across one of the windows before coming out of the door and getting into a van. I wonder what he's doing with a van on a farm but who knows—he may actually have good reason for it.

As he drives off, I tell Susan to follow and she does well, keeping back a subtle distance. The van heads towards Portree and as it comes to a stop on a corner. We sail past, and I see a number of hoodlums getting onboard. Taking the camera, I try and flash a few pictures, but the light's not great and to be honest I can't use anything like a flash which will give away my actions. With the speed of the car going past as well, they're not great pictures.

Susan turns around, tails back, and we pick up the van again on the move, as it the heads out towards a campsite just outside Portree. I see the van stop and watch with my binoculars as James McAvoy gets out, makes his way over to what looks like the administration block of the campsite. A middle-aged man comes out with him and steps into the back of the van. I notice he's carrying some sort of an envelope and as he gets back out again that envelope is missing. I think about going to the other man but there's no time as the van pulls off and soon, we're outside a hotel.

It seems busy enough. McAvoy goes in, and once again brings someone out. This time it's a middle-aged woman, dressed smartly in a skirt and jacket and she's also holding an envelope. As she steps inside the van, I wonder what it's like for her because there's a lot of hoods in there, primed and ready. I doubt they hold their tongue while she's in there, but she appears again two minutes later. Looking a little ruffled, she heads back inside but again there's no time to speak to her as the van pulls away.

The last stop is at a guest house and it is a reasonably large one, but has vacancies up in its window. There doesn't seem to be that many people about. McAvoy comes in to knock at the door and there's a young woman there, maybe about twenty-four or twenty-five. She seems to be having an argument with him and I see McAvoy look about which makes me nervous. My fears are realised when he grabs the back of her head, pulling her by the hair towards the van and throwing her inside.

I can hear the shock in Susan as she lets go an audible gasp, but I tell her to wait here and I step out of the car. I wonder how I should play this, because I may need to get close to that van to try and rescue her somehow if things are going wrong.

Instead I open the car door and say to Susan, 'Go and drive into that guesthouse, go up to the door and make out you're looking for somewhere to stay.' Susan nods, but gives me an anxious look, then drives off quickly, turning the car into the driveway while I hide down on the roadside. Fortunately, there's a ditch that runs along the side of the road and I make my way along it, crawling despite it being full of brambles. As I peer up over the top to see what's going on, I see Susan at the front door of the guest house, knocking on it and beginning to shout around for someone. The door of the van opens, but I can't see the woman from behind. She seems to speak to Susan briefly before turning around and walking back inside the van. There's nobody in the front of the van, everyone in the back so I jump up onto the road, run to the side of it, putting my ear next to it.

'If there's no payment next time, I'll let these boys loose on you.' It's McAvoy's voice and it sounds dark and sinister.

'You don't scare me. I don't care what you do, you don't scare me.' There's a bit of kerfuffle, something going on, and I hear a 'yelp' from the woman. Then comes the dark voice again of McAvoy.

'Okay, boys, I think she knows what you're going to play with next time.' I'd hate to find out what happened in there, because it certainly wasn't good. As the door slides open again, I hear McAvoy's voice saying, 'If you're lucky, they'll play with you—if not, it'll be me.'

The man gives me the creeps. God knows what he's doing to that woman. I hear her feet crunch as she walks up the drive to her house and I quickly sprint back to the roadside, jumping into the ditch. The van pulls away and once I see it's clear from sight, I jump out of the ditch and walk over to join Susan who's talking to the woman. The woman's wearing a skirt with a light blouse on top, but I notice it's ripped, several of the buttons are missing and she looks very agitated.

'Ma'am, I understand you're having some trouble.'

The woman looks at me, 'Who's this?' she says to Susan.

'This is my employer,' says Susan. 'I'm not really looking for accommodation and we're investigating what these people are doing. He's clearly threatened you and we'd like to help.'

Susan's getting particularly good at this and I decide to let her talk rather than produce a male voice at a time, which for the woman could be very stressful. Part of me wants to plant one right on McAvoy for what he's done to this woman today, letting those crappy hoods have a go at her.

'You can't help me,' she says. 'I'm getting out of here.'

'No,' says Susan, 'don't; just stay here. We'll protect you if he comes back next time.' It's a turn up for the books and one I wasn't expecting, but it could be good.

'I'll protect you,' I say, 'but I want something as well. I take it you have a phone number for him? I want you to bring him back here tonight, but later, when he's on his own. Give him an indication that you might be able to, and I know you're not going to like what I'm about to say, give him some favours, to overlook the payments.'

You can see the woman shudder.

'But don't worry, I'm not asking you to do that. I'm only

wanting him back here and then I will deal with him. You need to understand, he's in trouble too, and he's not the real person behind all of this. He's just the one you see.' I ask the woman to go inside, which she does, and I suggest she goes to change because it can't be good sitting in a top that she's just been abused in.

The guesthouse itself is delightful; she's laid the whole thing out nicely and there's fresh flowers there, everywhere. Everything looks spick and span but there's nobody here.

When she comes back downstairs, we find out her story, and why she's on Skye. It turns out her fiancée died two years ago and this is her getaway to start up again. In a lot of ways, she's very plain looking but for that, like most people of youth, she has that warmth about her and I reckon deep down there's an incredibly positive person to start up again. To get yourself out here and begin a business, that takes something, especially after losing what you thought was the love of your life.

'Have you gone to the police about this?' I ask, and she says she was visited by a Sergeant. He said they were struggling to do anything about it and that she hadn't given him enough evidence. I ask if she called it in on the normal police line, but she says no. He actually visited after the first time she was threatened, in the area, paying visits.

'On his own,' I query, 'because that sounds extremely unusual.' I ask did she get a name for him and she says it was Gillespie. She also says that when she was to ring up if she ever needed to again, she was only to ask for him as he was the one dealing with all of this. It's absolutely breath-taking the way they're running this, and the fact that the man sitting right in front of me as if he knew nothing in that coffee shop this afternoon.

The woman makes a call and it's heading towards twilight

and McAvoy appears. This time he's not in his van, but instead in his own car and as he comes up to the house, the woman goes outside waving him closer. Her name is Anna and I had a word with her so she's now standing outside in a dressing gown, with plenty of bare legs showing. I made the point that she needed to do this so that McAvoy thought she was serious. I also thought given McAvoy's form, that any chance to be with a woman was going to resonate with him.

He makes his way up the drive as instructed. Now I need to get him inside where it will be easier to contain him. She lets him come up to her and puts her hand out, taking his and walks inside the door, telling him to make his way through to the living room. She's nervous and shaking, but that's good because he would expect it to be like that anyway.

As he walks into the living room, I club him hard right in the back of the head and he falls to the ground. I then threw two quick boots into him and he clutches at his guts. Grabbing him by the hair, I drag him up and throw him into a chair. I give him another punch to the stomach, causing him to double up before pulling his head back and Susan begins to tie him up. I quickly search him, once he's been tied, but he has nothing on him, probably expecting just to come along here and have his way quickly before heading home.

'Your game's up, McAvoy. I know what you've been doing.' But as I'm about to continue, a hand comes on my shoulder. It's Anna and she asks me to step aside a moment. I move out of the way cautiously wondering what she's about to do. She lets go an almighty slap to the man's face.

'That's for threatening me.' she says. She then disappears out of the room. I turn back, telling the man he deserved it, before she appears again, and gently moves me out of the way.

111

'Do you know what this is?' she says, holding it up close to his face. It's got a plastic handle, a metal shaft and then like a large lump on the end with some minor markings coming off it. 'This is a mace,' she spits. 'We use it when we go fishing. We take the fish out, we whack them with it, and we kill it straight away.'

I'm starting to get nervous. She really doesn't think she's going to take him out?

'Open your legs,' she says. The man shakes his head, so she yells at him to open his legs. I understand what she's about to do, but she'll never get a decent swing in the position he's sitting. Normally, I wouldn't go for this sort of thing; it's actually a distraction, but when I saw her for the first time, she was getting hands laid on her and not in any good way. So, I nod to Susan and I reach down and grab one knee myself, watching Susan grab the other. It takes Anna about ten seconds and the man cries out in pain.

'That's enough, Anna. I need him to be able to do things after this, though I can fully understand why you'd want to rip him apart.'

'No, you don't,' she says. And yes, she's probably right, not to the extent that she understands, but I need him.

'You bitch,' he cries. 'You bloody bitch.' He's still trying to double over in pain, but he's tied up and cannot move, and damn, it must hurt.

'Listen up, sunshine,' I say. 'We're going to sit and have a talk about how you're going to help us, and you're going to help us because any refusal or any indication in the next hour that you're not helping us and I'm going out of this room, but not before I've tied your legs in a position where she can sit and play with that mace all day long.

'And I'll stay too,' says Susan. 'I won't need a mace.'

I'm quite astonished at the violence that came out of her mouth, but I get it and if anything, she's gone a little bit Hollywood with it. But the man sees that I'm for real with the fact that I'll leave him to these women. When he looks up, he sees Anna looking straight at him, teeth bared, almost snarling at him. She went through the death of her partner, built a new life for herself up here only to have these people try and take it away. She's obviously been abused and still holding out. The man must be crapping himself because if I leave her in here, he's not going to have anything to go home with.

'You going to be a good boy for him?' asks Anna. The man nods.

'Right, then,' I say, 'let's get started.'

Chapter Fourteen

McAvoy is trying to play the hardman, looking up at me with steeled eyes but his shoulders don't cut the mustard. I can see them shaking, can see the tension running through his body. I can guess he's scared witless; whether that's of me or whether it's of Anna, here in the room with me, I don't know. But of course, it could also be that he's scared of Jenny Carnegie and her people and what they might do to him if they find out he's been taken in like this.

'What's your relationship with Jenny Carnegie?' I say, in a very matter of fact way. The man looks up at me, spits onto the carpet of the house.

'I don't know who you're talking about.' I watch Anna's eyes; she looks at the carpet and walks over to the man and delivers him a thumping slap across the face.

'I think she's asking that you don't mess up the carpet,' I say, 'and stop lying. I know you gather at the Fairy Pools. I've seen you stand there while she dances and then she whispers something in your ear. I know you're on the rounds, going up to different hotels, with a bunch of hoods and I believe I've met them as well. What's the deal here, McAvoy? Are you just a hardman? How does she know you? How are you involved?

What's your cut?'

His eyes widen; they did as soon as I mentioned Jenny Carnegie.

'It's nothing for you to worry about, just a little racket here; it's because some people can't behave themselves.' His eyes stares at Anna and she looks back fiercely. I really don't know who he's got more worries about, me or her.

'How did you get involved with her?' I ask. And he just turns his head away. It dawns on me then how he got into this whole mess, and actually it's pretty obvious when you have watched him for a bit. 'Where did she seduce you? Was your Mrs around at the time? Did she film it? Put a bit of blackmail on you? You're a big guy, maybe you're what she needed. A bit of muscle, someone to keep rowdy troops in order and you got a bit of an estate up there. Is that when you got into the holiday-making trade? And you start putting out those other bits of accommodation.' He says nothing, but it's pretty obvious that I'm at least reasonably on the money.

'And with a wife at home as well, and kids running around, cheating on her. I've been tailing you for a while and I've got a lot I can dump to on the police so they'll come straight to you. But I don't want you, McAvoy, I want Jenny Carnegie. I want her locked up because she's the one pushing this. And I want to know when something big is going down. We're going to take a bit of footage here, of you talking to us, telling us all about what's happening. And when I have that, you're going to go and you're going to be a good boy for me. You're going to ring me when something's happening, and we're going to bring these people down. But in the meantime, you're going to leave Anna here alone because if I find you've laid a finger on her, I'll put you in this seat and I'll let her take the knacker's off you.'

That's not actually something that I'm going to do, but I try and play the part at least. I'm also not going to film him. And he's certainly not going to be filmed talking with me. That kind of thing counts as evidence against me and says that I actually forcibly held someone, so generally I tend not to store anything that can't be plausibly denied by anyone else. If he comes back and says that I was held like this, Susan will tell everybody where I was—Anna here, too. It's not a difficult scheme to run. But as soon as you put stuff on electronics, as soon as you actually physically record something and put it down, that can disappear and end up somewhere else.

If he says, but I was watching him the whole time, I'm a private investigator, it's my job. And I've also got a record of why I'm doing it and why I'm looking at everyone else. But no, if I go a little bit beyond, I certainly don't make a physical note of it.

'Is there anyone lined up today, for a proper beating? Like you tried to deliver the other day with the hoods. Did they tell you someone was in there, someone with one arm, a freak? That was me, and these ribs are smarting, so you better make sure you come back with something good.'

He looks at me, his eyes angry, but he knows he's beat here. He knows he's got nowhere to go.

'And stay off the drink,' I say. 'Doesn't do me any good if you crash your quad again.' His eyes look up in rage, and he realizes I've got tabs on him everywhere. 'You already are in debt for this one, McAvoy, so be a good boy; you never know—you might get to spend most of the time still with your kids. And don't worry, we'll make it out that Anna here is selling up. You've done a good job, so just get close.' I go to turn away but then I spin back, I go right into the man's face.

'I've seen plenty of this, plenty of people used like yourself and it angers me, what might have been a decent family man, ends up like this. But what really angers me is you go beyond. You don't just bring the boys around for a few words, you actually enjoy it and come in here looking for your desserts, looking for extras for yourself. That's when you lost me, sunshine. You'd better play this one right by the book, make sure I'll drop you in it to Jenny. Yeah, 'I say, as he realizes, I'm not talking about the police, 'I'll drop you right in it with her. I'm sure you won't last long.'

Untying him, he goes to make for Anna, but I put a hand on a shoulder, 'It all gets dropped right in Jenny's lap. Go and find me something, something juicy. And I want it soon, okay? '

The man turns around and nods. And he gives a last stare at Anna.

'No,' I say, 'you don't look at her like that way any time again—you don't even as much as think of her. Understood?' The man nods and I send him out of the house.

When I go back into the living room, Anna's sitting down with Susan beside her, holding her hand.

'You think that worked?' she asks. 'Will he leave me alone?'

'Yes, but you need to make inquiries. You need to phone up somewhere, some solicitor, anything, and talk about moving. You won't be doing it, but you need to talk about it, you need to give the impression while I get this sorted for you.'

'Is it definitely going to work?' she says.

'I hope so because if it doesn't, they'll be after me as well. We'll see what information he comes back with, and if there's not enough for me to act, we'll get onto the police with it. But I need to be careful—there may be the odd policemen involved in this as well.'

Anna looks at me shocked, 'So we're stuffed then, if we go that way?'

'Sergeant Gillespie visited and told you nothing could be done, and I think that's because he's the one, certainly the bad apple on the side of the police. But I don't know if there's more. I'll have to see.'

I take Susan aside. 'Have a look at the rest of the establishments in the area, find out about them, but also, I want you to keep an eye here on Anna. Check in with her. Anything wrong, message me. If she's looking a bit peaky, but if you're worried that she's going to do something, take her with you, just so you look like you're two girls on a day out. And watch your back,' I say. 'Anything untoward, you drive the car off Skye, and you keep driving to Stranraer and just message me, okay?'

Susan nods and I go over to shake the hand of Anna. I can see why a woman like her would interest someone like McAvoy; you can see why she would interest anyone. I think there's a strength inside her, something that can stand up to this, but that takes time and it takes a toll. Even when she was in the van, she didn't flinch so she's made of some strong sort of stuff. I want to make sure she doesn't have to display that kind of fortitude again. It makes me sick, especially after the early loss she's had in her life. The last thing she needs is something like that when she's missing where her deceased lover would have been.

Leaving both women, I make my way back to Portree and take the tender back to Craigantlet. As I step onboard, Martha comes up on deck. She's wearing a large floppy jumper and she steps across the boat in an unsure way, as she always does when not on land, before giving me a hug.

'You're looking good,' I say.

But her eyes are full of concern, and she whispers in my ear, 'You don't want her here. She's a killer—you did right having me around.' I take Martha to the far end of the boat, whispering to her about what's happened, bringing her up to speed with my plans. When we descend back down into the cabin, Maggie comes over to embrace me, and I see that Jenny Carnegie has made herself comfortable, sitting on one of the side benches of the main cabin. She's wearing a long shirt, but her legs are bare and I can see Maggie's face because it's obvious the woman is flaunting herself again. I put my arm around Maggie, just to reassure her. Well, I think, she has no need to be reassured. When have I ever stepped out of the line?

'Well, we're making progress,' I say. 'I think we've got McAvoy on our side and pretty soon we should be able to move properly but until then, I'd like you to stay on the boat, Jenny. I don't think it's safe for you back on the land yet.'

She runs a hand up, along one of her legs, then looks up to me. 'It's not a bad place to stay. I feel a bit more safe and secure here.'

I turn round and ask Maggie and Martha if they could pop up top and just give me a moment. I see Maggie's face as they do.

'You need to stay here, Jenny,' I say. 'We need to look after you,' and I sit down beside her, with her hand up along her leg.

'I do feel safe here,' she says, as she adjusts her shirt, making sure I can see plenty.

'Good,' I say. She leans forward and starts to kiss me right on the lips. I pretend to pull away before letting her kiss me properly. Then I break off and put a finger up to my mouth. 'Keep it quiet; we'll get Maggie off the boat soon enough.'

119

That evening as we retire to bed, Jenny's lying in the cabin, Martha in the smaller room near the front of the boat, and Maggie and myself are in the main cabin. I can feel an uneasiness in Maggie.

'What?' I say, whispering quietly into her ear. 'What's the matter?' My single arm wraps around her.

'You know she wants you.'

'No, she doesn't,' I say, 'and all of this flaunting and flirting is to buy me in. She's a player and she's allowed herself to be brought here to find out what I'm about and what I know. But I'm making her work for that. She thinks I'm finally buying into her. I told her you'd be disappearing off the boat soon enough.' I feel Maggie shake slightly. 'Don't worry you won't, there's no way I'd leave myself or you alone with her. That's why Martha's here. The more I find out about her, the more I think I shouldn't have left you with her in the first place, but we're committed now and I need to see this through. So just stay with it, because while I've got her camped down here, I can put more pressure on other bits of the organization that she's running until I can get to a point where I can just drop them all in it. Might be a couple of days, Maggie, hopefully no longer.'

'Just be careful,' she says. 'I don't trust her. You don't come into the spider's den willingly. If she faked that accident, like you say, she wants to be here and if she wants to be here, that can't be good.

'I agree but when you see what these people are doing, you understand why I can't let it go.' And I recount to her about what happened to Anna that day. 'And this woman is okay with that, okay with women being abused, being forced and coerced, okay, with making this rather unstable guy go through all of this, bringing out his nasty side. So, we need to shut it down because I already know the story of one of those guys but of all of those that meet in that circle, she's got to be using them in a similar way.'

She cuddles behind me, arms around my thigh. 'Just be careful,' she says. 'I don't want to end up like Anna.'

'You won't. Besides, Martha's on the scene now, and she doesn't take crap from anybody.'

I hear a giggle from Maggie. 'You're right there; she's taken over the boat since she arrived. She can move pretty quick for such a big woman.'

'You've no idea what she's like. And if you ever watched her on a laptop, you'll see how sharp she really is.' Everything goes quiet and I hear the gentle lap of the water against the boat. I'm starting to drift off, when Maggie rolls over, facing me, and wraps herself around me.

'Just take care.'

Chapter Fifteen

I wake up in the morning and that reassuring side of the boat, gently getting hit by the water, is there again. It's one of the things I love about being a sailor—that easy motion. The other thing I'm loving at the moment is the fact that I'm not waking up alone and my arm's still snaked around Maggie, but it's a sound from inside the cabin I hear first. The door slides back that leads through to the bunk and I see Jenny Carnegie stepping out. There's not a lot left to the imagination; she does have a shirt on. She's making her way across to my shower; it's fairly compact on the boat, as you can imagine. I watch her disappear inside it, to re-emerge five minutes later, her wet hair is hanging down her back and the shirt's now damp in places as she goes and sits opposite the bunk that I'm lying on with Maggie. Maggie's fast asleep and leaning in towards me. I know what Jenny's doing and I play along, giving her a smile, letting her think that she's in with me. And then Maggie comes alive with a start.

'What?' she says.

'We've got company.'

'Sorry,' says Jenny, 'I didn't mean to intrude, I'll just get out of the way,' and with that, she walks back to the bunk room, the shirt swinging, revealing plenty.

'Some woman,' I say out loud, for Jenny's benefit. I get a dig in the ribs from Maggie. 'I'm play-acting,' I whisper.

'I can't believe you enjoy that view,' she says.

'Of course, you can,' I say, 'but it's not the view that matters, is it? You're more than a view, Maggie. I hope you know that.' I may have been cheesy, but I guess I hit the right tone because she cuddles right up into me.

About an hour later, everyone's dressed and changed and I'm sitting up on deck with Martha. The day's warm, but Martha's still wearing a large baggy sweater.

'Did your volleyball ever work out?' I ask.

'Yeah,' she says, 'still going to it, still fun. A couple of nice people go to it as well.'

'All right,' I say, 'anyone really nice?'

'Like I'd tell you,' she says, and that tells me that there is.

'Well, good for you, but what about what I'm paying you for?'

She grins, 'There's large number of irregularities going on, Paddy. There's money changing hands into smaller companies here, withdrawals being made by a number of companies. I'm working through it but I can see that the cash is being taken out on too regular a basis; it's hinting at extortion, at people having to hand over money to keep businesses afloat. The difficulty is trying to trace that cash because I don't think they're putting it into any local bank. It's going away elsewhere. How they're laundering it, I don't know.

'Well, keep on it,' I say. 'As soon as you can trace the money, it's easier to hand this all in. In the meantime, I'll try and get some more physical evidence.'

I spend the rest of the day on the boat mainly because I haven't got anywhere to go. I let Susan run around, checking into hotels. She calls me twice, saying that Anna's come with her, because the woman is feeling a bit scared on her own and frankly, I don't blame her. I say to Susan, 'I'll meet you this evening and I'll leave about seven o'clock.'

I try to take my leave of Craigantlet, but Maggie comes up to me. 'She's asking for you in there. She was making out it was quite urgent.'

Martha's on the end of the boat, sitting with her laptop, and I say to Maggie to just wait up here. I can see the look on her face. 'Don't worry, I'm just playing along.'

Descending into the cabin, I find Jenny Carnegie looking at one of the portholes and she's dressed again in that shirt, her long legs exposed and with one finger raised, she calls me over. I reach my arm around her and she takes it with both arms pulling me close.

'How long to get her off the boat?' she asks.

'Easy, we can't be too cautious,' I reply. 'I need to have good reason for her to go somewhere and it's not happened yet. Besides, there'll be plenty of time once I get this sorted. What's your rush?'

'You know what my rush is,' she says, and turns around so she's directly in front of me. With all the calmness that you would grant an actress, she reaches up, pulls her shirt apart, and lets it drop.

This is leaving me in a rather sticky situation because while I said to Maggie, I was playing along, I didn't realize Jenny would play it like this, standing there, basically in her pants. This is isn't going to do my relationship with Maggie a lot of good if she walks in. The shirt hangs on the elbows of her arm and I reach forward, lay my hand around her back, tracing it up and down, once or twice before I grab the top of the shirt and pull it back up and gently cover her up.

'Later. You go too quick, we'll blow this completely.'

It must be annoying her like anything, because I'm sure a lot of men must melt at her charms, especially when she offers herself like that. But if I'm honest, something behind it feels vile. Like any man, I enjoy the view. But like I said to Maggie, you don't just come for the view, you come for the place and if the place isn't any good, you certainly wouldn't stay. You don't want to be looking at that view, with all the filth around you.

I go back up on deck and see Maggie's worried face. I tell her, 'In case you're wondering, she did try. But don't worry, you still got this silly old Irishman.' She smiles. 'But she did try, bigtime!' There's annoyance in Maggie's face, but at least it's aimed in the right direction and not at me. 'Stay calm, stay safe, let Martha handle things.'

I get a quick kiss before I'm on the tender, making my way over to the harbour and then into my car. I meet Susan in the recesses of a local bar as she sits with her diet coke and I with my cup of tea, a few locals look at us as if we just don't know how to have fun.

'I've been to several places, Paddy, mostly in and around Portree. A lot of them are full up. From the ones that are fully booked, you get nothing. You get no complaints, nothing. It's like everything's perfect. As the others when you start talking about business, they clam up and tell you they don't want to talk about that sort of thing. Then they start to telling you how hard the climate is here because of factors. But there's been one particular establishment I was in.

'He was a man of about forty and when I went to see him, he wanted to talk. I don't think he was worried about what was happening, I think he just liked me, so he fancied talking to me for a while. When he came here, he said he was just about able to buy the place. It was meant to be being taken up by other people, but whatever happened, the other person fell through. He says it was rather a bad time for them because of it, and two months later, they met with a bad accident on the road.

'But he bought the place and he said that someone came round about three weeks later saying that a lot of people here had trouble and they could organize it so the trouble would go away. He said he laughed at him. But the guy said that they had a special list you could get on to, a list that would help bring the guests in, regular guests at good prices and the fee wasn't that expensive.

'The guy knew what it was all about, Paddy. I mean, this owner was smart, and he said they roughed him up a couple of times too. But he said he's made his own path into bringing people here, because he's leaning to a very particular type of client. He didn't say who and I didn't ask but apparently, that's why he's full. He said when they found out what sort of people he had in, they weren't interested.'

I ask her what sort of people they are, and Susan says it's like some sort of a group; everyone seems to be mismatched, not the correct ages. I reckon it could be some sort of lonely-hearts thing, set up separately, but not just for getting together and saying hello.

'Sort of a sex holiday,' she says, 'but not with like working girls or anything, just one on the quiet.'

'Well, if they forced that guy out and things got into the papers, that's not the publicity you want for your tourist haven, is it? Maybe that's why they've left him alone. Did he say how they came in to threaten him?'

'At the last place,' she says, 'he said a lot of youth turned up in a van.'

'We need to find out where those hoodlums are from, but carefully, because if those boys get you alone, well, you know what'll happen. So, don't dig too deep unless you're able to get out somewhere.'

Susan smiles at me, but behind it is a solemnness. She realizes the risk she takes at times. Quite often I'm just open to a good beating, but being a woman, there's other things they could do to her. It's not pretty, but, hey, it's the filth I mix amongst. You don't become a private investigator and get to investigate nice people.

'I'll have a look, see what I can dig up. Have you had any word yet?' she asks.

'No, Mr. McAvoy's been very quiet, if he doesn't contact me by tomorrow, I may pay another visit. There's a lot going on. I mean, he was taking a van around, on his weekly collections. Martha can't trace everything through yet. She knows there's money being taken out of bank accounts, but it's not going back in and it's going out to cash, so they're storing it somewhere. I'll try and work on that, but for the meantime, keep it low key, keep it safe, see if you can find out where those boys are, and see if you can get the names of any more establishments that are having trouble.'

Susan nods at me, 'Okay. Oh, by the way, I got a message from Mum earlier on; are you all right? She said your guest was messing with you.'

'Messing with me, is that how she should put it,' and I explain to Susan what Jenny Carnegie's is up to. 'But your mother doesn't have to worry—we're just playing along, putting out the bait.'

We finish our drinks and Susan heads off back to her new hotel and I head back to Craigantlet. As I reach the harbour and get into the tender, it's a lovely night, the water calm and I can see Maggie up on top of the boat. As I arrive, she helps me up and we secure the tender. Before I can go downstairs, she takes hold of me, leading me to the end of the boat, forcing me to sit down and hold her as she sits between my legs.

'Martha told me to tell you, Jenny Carnegie's got a phone and she's been using it. Martha is trying to listen in, but she can't find out much. Said the woman's generally texting but Martha can't intercept it. She's planning something. You probably want to get down there, see if you can extract a little more information from her.'

I wrap my arm around Maggie and pull her close, 'No, I don't. She's making her move. I'm going to give her the cold shoulder, wait till she comes to me because then anything she's telling me, I know, it's for the benefit of whatever plan she's concocting and not for her personal enjoyment.'

'You think she's enjoying you, while she's trying to do this?'

I pull Maggie close. 'Well, you seem to enjoy me.'

She laughs, turns around and together we lie on top of the boat, having a moment. 'I wish we were back, just the two of us, sailing around,' says Maggie. 'All this work keeps getting in the way. You need to wrap these cases up a lot quicker,' she teases.

And then we hear the door open and somebody begins to come out on deck. I see Maggie's face and I know it's not Martha. Maggie gets off me and I roll around. I give a husky voice saying, 'Get inside,' to Jenny. She's up in just a shirt. It's buttoned up but all the same, she's not meant to be seen up on deck. I walk quickly over escorting her back down to the cabin, where she takes my arm.

'I'm just worried. I'm worried and I need somebody close.

Do you think you could come to the bunk tonight?'

'No,' I say, 'it's too risky. I need to keep up the pretence.' And with that, I make my way back up on deck, to an awaiting Maggie, who gives me an embrace.

'I hope you've been cruel to her,' she says.

'Totally, but don't be surprised if we get a visit in the middle of the night.'

Chapter Sixteen

As I'm lying in bed, I get the call. It's a simple text on my phone, not my normal phone, but the phone I gave to McAvoy for contact. Maggie stirs and I pull it across and start looking at it. McAvoy says he wants to meet now, which at four in the morning is a little bit desperate. But, if I want to find out what's going on, this is what I have to do.

So, I get up, get changed, before stopping at the door quickly for Maggie to give me a hug and a kiss goodbye. Then I get into the tender and make my way across. The daylight is creeping in and McAvoy wants to meet in Portree. His place of choice is down a side alley, which fills me with a little bit of apprehension. But I arrive around twenty minutes before the time to meet, to make sure no one's about. I wouldn't put it past him to arrange the thugs to turn up and give me a seeing to.

As I'm waiting for McAvoy, I think of how I got started on this. Ingrid Appleton coming along asking about her husband, where he was going. Susan has been the main point of contact for her giving brief updates. But with the way things are, it was explained to her that she had to stay in the dark, yet I don't think Ingrid's in on it. I think Ingrid is the woman who saw something going wrong with her husband. However, that's not the case with Jenny's husband.

I'm standing in the alley as McAvoy comes around the corner. He's on his own and he's looking furtively here, there, and everywhere. He makes his way quickly up to me.

'It's going to happen tonight,' he says. They got in touch with me, left a note through my door. Normally you get to meet but she's not about. Not able to get to the pools. So, a note came, signed by her as well.

I know that's a lie because she's on my boat, but then again, how does he know what her handwriting looks like? And I also think it's a bit reckless communicating like that. But then again, if she is instructing him to do things, he has to know it's genuine somehow.

'Where is it?' I ask.

'Outside of Portree, on the road towards Duntulm,' he says. 'Go beyond by about half a mile and you'll see the Kingfisher Hotel. They're going to burn it to the ground.'

'Why?' I say. 'What have they done wrong?'

'New English couple that came in,' says McAvoy. 'Apparently, they haven't been paying up. She seems to have little patience. Possibly threaten them to go somewhere else. She says that they have to be thrown out.'

'What's going to happen?'

'The boys will go round, set fire to the place. Just as they are coming through the door, scare the bejesus out of them. Then move them on so we can get another punter in.'

'Are you sure it's going to be them?'

'I told you, she sent a letter. It's signed. It's what I have to do. So, I'm away to sort out the boys, explain their business to them.'

'Where are you going to be?' I ask. 'Are you making the hit with them?'

'I'm normally in the vicinity,' says McAvoy. 'But I don't normally do it. If they get caught, they get caught. They don't know anything about what's up above me. All they know is they get a package of money. Thugs, really. Sitting around doing nothing—just pays for their beer money.'

It strikes me as funny that he's got such a bad opinion of them considering what he's doing himself. Beating his wife, extorting money out of people and yet thinks he's using lazy dropouts. People's opinions of other people never cease to amaze me, especially amongst the criminal fraternity.

'Just go along and act normal,' I say. 'I'll be the one on the other end sorting things out.'

I watch as the man walks off. I try to judge if he's bluffing but everything seems normal. He appears down in the dumps like he's been forced, which he is. But at least I've got a contact.

I make a call to Susan and get her up out of her bed to meet her for breakfast. We're back at the cafe we were in a few days ago and Susan makes the most of my visit. Sitting down to a full cooked breakfast, I guess the work must be tiring her because she's normally a fairly healthy eater. As for me today, I just have some scrambled eggs. There's part of me feels tense inside because something's going to happen tonight that could go very, very wrong.

'I want you to be watching from a distance,' I say. 'I'll get close trying and take the photographs, but I want you at a distance in case anything goes wrong. You can highlight the relevant people. Don't mess about—call 999—tell them exactly what's happening. We'll also have to make sure we're properly undercover, so change the car. I'll leave separately, but you can drive me close. And then I'll get out and work from there. It's not going to be dark so we need you to be someone else, something that changes your look. Don't go silly with a baseball hat and dark glasses on or you'll just look like a suspect.'

She giggles and then suddenly her face becomes serious. 'They're going to set fire to the place, Paddy—that could go bad. We really should be warning these people.'

'I know,' I say, 'but this is how we get the evidence. It's what is going to stitch him up and once we've got him by the short and curlies, hopefully, we can make it go up the line. She's left herself open with a note anyway informing him about the hit. Telling him to set it up—that goes right back to Jenny. With that in our pocket, I think we can make the call to the police, get them involved. It all seems to be straightforward.'

There's a doubt in my head. Something's nagging me. I still don't understand why she's come onto to my boat. Why she wants to look at what an investigator is doing. Surely, the thing is to keep them at a distance, not get them involved. Or does she seriously think that I am something.

'I reckon something's wrong,' says Susan. 'From where I'm sitting, I don't understand why she's on that boat with you telling me she's made advances at you as well. Why? Just to simply find out what you know? Why not just scare you off? How well does she know you? Is your reputation here ahead of you? Most of the time it has been me doing the following around. You also said her husband doesn't need to find out what's going on; something's not right, Paddy.'

'I agree.'

I sip my coffee. I also don't know why she's running around with that landowner as well. What I want to keep close so I can get another look into that and find out what that relationship is. Something's not right here but I don't have enough to go to the police with.

I spend the afternoon back on the boat. When I tell Jenny, I have to go out that night, she doesn't seem too perturbed, though she does try to catch me alone inside the bunk cabin. But I stay out of the way because I know it's a strain on Maggie.

Martha has been finding more and more people who seem to be struggling to fill their holiday spaces, but she's still struggling to trace the money and thinking it may not actually be put away anywhere yet. Maybe they're hiding it in a hole.

'Maybe it's to going to drifting into a completely different venture,' she says, 'but they've got cash lying around and if we could find it, we'll blow them wide open with that. One thing to be aware of is that if you do find it, Jenny might make a run for it off the boat.'

I confirm that Martha is armed, and that she'll take no risks, not with Maggie on board. 'Just play it cool and calm, if she makes a run for it.'

The trip back over in the tender is on another perfect evening with hardly a ripple in the water. I drive my car to Susan's hotel, back in Kyle before we make the trip back over in Susan's new rental vehicle. Making our way across Skye, we find the hotel. It's down by a river, nestled nicely on the side giving only one access into it. Which means that if they set fire to it, they're blocking the only way out. I wonder how they will do this. Will there be a warning, or will they set the fire in such a way that anyone inside can get out? If needs be, I might have to run in and warn everyone.

It's ten at night and the traffic in the area has slowed down. I wonder how long they will wait before making their attack. I send Susan out skirting around, looking for them, but she sees no signs. She does a quick recce up to McAvoy's house and his car is missing. When she returns, I send her a little

134

way off from myself. She texts me that she thinks something is wrong. We're now at midnight and no one's moved, no one's come near, even the real darkness has started to settle in.

Saying that, it's not true darkness, it's still the twilight, and I can easily see anyone arriving. The rooms in the hotel have lights that are going out, people retiring off to bed, and the roads are almost silent. I see someone approach, a youngish lad walking towards the front door, so I head through the hedgerows, getting close to see what he's doing. He's got a bottle in his hand and I wonder if it's got something inside it which he can set fire to. From this distance, it looks like there might be a rag in the top.

He's got a cigarette in his mouth, and I wonder if he'll light it from that. As he gets up to the front door, he sways unsteadily, banging on the door and shouting for Anna Marie.

I don't know who Anna Marie is, but if he's meant to be setting fire to this building, he is going the wrong way about it. Eventually someone comes to the door, possibly the owners, telling him to clear off. When they return inside, I watch him turn away briefly before making his way back to the door. He opens up the letterbox and I wait to see him pour the fuel in.

But he doesn't. He unzips his fly and urinates in through the door. Something's not right here. I text Susan asking if she's seen anyone else. The reply comes back negative. I take a scout around the building, running quickly, but there's no one there. When I return to the front from a position in the hedgerow, I see the door open. The guy is still there, fly still undone and I can hear the swearing of the owner as they come out through the door. There's a bit of a scuffle, nothing serious, before the drunken man falls to the ground. It's not a pretty sight and I'm sure somebody is going to be calling the police soon.

I trudged wearily back to the car. Susan looks at me, bemused. She thinks that it might be later or maybe it's got called off. Definitely so if the police arrive. It's only two minutes later when they drive in and I see them start to search the ground around the house. I realize I made a great move in getting myself back inside the car.

'Where to then, Paddy?' Susan says, and I shake my head.

'I don't know, Susan, I really don't know. Maybe McAvoy scuppers us, maybe he doesn't care anymore. Maybe they told him, maybe he said to them. I don't know. I thought I had him in my pocket, but maybe I don't. I'll figure it out tomorrow, find out what went wrong. But we'll see anyway. I think I'll stay in the car and see if anyone arrives from here, rather than hanging out in that hedge.'

Susan laughs, 'Well, at least you are getting the rubbish end of the job,' she says.

'Don't start or you'll be on hedgerow duty next.' I nudge her with my elbow, but she says nothing because she's looking through the rear-view mirror of the car park.

'Paddy, there's a bloody massive blaze behind us. Look!' I spin round in the seat and look through the small rear screen window. I can see an orange glow in the sky.

'Go,' I say, 'just go get there.'

Susan floors the car down the road giving it all she's worth. As she comes to a long driveway leading up to a hotel, she's nearly hit by the van, driving out the other way. She goes to turn around, but I tell her to keep driving towards the blaze as I dial 999.

'Which service do you require?'

'Fire service?'

A few seconds later, there's a female voice on the other end asking what the emergency is. I tell her whereabouts we are roughly on Skye. She's looking for a more detailed answer, but she can't miss it, the only bloody big bonfire around here. I tell her, I'm going to make sure the building's clear, but she insists I don't. Tells me to wait for the fire service. No way, I think, if people are in there.

As Susan pulls up in front of the hotel, it's now fully ablaze, and I jump out of the car with Susan screaming after me. I hold my jacket up as I run in through the front door. Glass shatters and around the reception area is blazing bright. As I look through into the dining room, I shout loudly for anyone to get out. I make my way up a flight of stairs and start banging on room doors. I can't find anyone up there and as I go downstairs, I hear a scream.

It seems to be coming from behind the door that's furthest along from the main door I entered in by. As I get there, I read the placard that says 'Office' on the door. But the door is stuck. There's a woman inside screaming so I kick hard at the door several times. Nothing happens. Again, the woman screams. I turn around, run across the corridor, flames around me. Finally, I'm starting to choke. The smoke is filling this corridor and I need to get into the room quick or I'll start to succumb to the fire. I run forward, pitching my shoulder down and throw myself full tilt.

As I lie crumpled, a man leans over to me and asks me, 'Is there anyone inside?'

'Yes, I saw one person in the office. But I think she succumbed; she went under a pile of debris.

I hear them running back and forward, starting to get hoses together, men in masks with big tanks on their back, trying to make an entry. Ten minutes later, an ambulance arrives, and they come over to us, I assume, because there's nobody else to deal with. There's a mask put over my face, probably to help me breathe more easily. But all I can do is stare at the hotel and the blazing fire. And to my mind comes the image of the woman. If you want to know, she was blonde haired. I'd say fifty. And her eyes, the most fearful I've ever seen. I've never known her, I mean, not even given her name. But one thing I can tell you is, she is a woman I will never forget.

Chapter Seventeen

There was quite a circus at the hotel with firemen, policemen, ambulance. All very necessary but it all seemed like a lot of bees moving about their hive around me while I sat there feeling numb and cold. The woman's face comes back to haunt me through most of that day. I've seen people die. I usually haven't had a chance to save them, but this was different, and she was there right in front of me.

They find her body eventually, once the fire was put down, and her husband's too. The police ask me and Susan what we were doing, and I tell them we were passing. At that time of the morning, it seems a little strange but I say we were out gathering nature, looking at stuff in those early hours. It seems to fit because we were really dressed to be outdoors.

He insists we go to hospital to get checked out, and I would except for how things are. I place a call to Maggie who was first of all concerned because she had not seen the news, and then secondly, rather angry because we hadn't phoned. I don't say on the phone, but if I'm honest, I'm a little bit shell shocked throughout the morning.

I decide to head back to the boat once I drop Susan off at her hotel, pick Maggie up and take her down to Susan. She is worried, and needs to see her daughter. And frankly, I don't want to be sitting on a boat with that woman because I don't think I can keep up my image. She killed someone, in fact, she killed two people because the husband was in there too. He was the one she'd gone for. He was the reason she hadn't gotten out.

After giving me an initial tirade of not ringing and keeping her informed, and explaining how she would feel if it was me inside that burning hotel, along with Susan, Maggie calmed down enough to simply hold me. But she can see that my mind is elsewhere, shocked, frozen. We hadn't slept through the night, so it is the back end of afternoon by the time I rise and take a shower.

'What happened?' said Maggie, 'I thought you knew where it was.'

'He lied to us,' I say, 'lied through his teeth.'

There's no way I could get it wrong. He was the one who was organizing them to do it. He was the one—he was getting the hoodlums together. He'd been instructed to and somebody else got there first, somebody else stepped in.

'Do you think she knew on the boat?' Martha says. 'She was communicating with them? Where does she sit in all this?'

'I don't know,' I say. 'But I'm holding on to her with Martha, first of all, because we need to go and find our informant. McAvoy could be in trouble. In fact, we should have moved by night. Damn it. Maggie, I should have moved. I just can't help seeing that face. I just can't help it.'

She wraps her arms around me. 'Quiet. It doesn't help, you need to think, you need to think what to do. Now focus on what's happened. Push aside, there'll be time for others to be in trouble. You need to think, Paddy.'

'We need to get you back,' I say. Maggie looks little shocked. 'She doesn't know what we are dealing with over here. As far as she's concerned, you've come over here to help find me new clothing, other things to look at, helping me with stuff. I need to get you back. I need to get her thinking things are normal. Not that I'm scampering off looking for a missing farmer.'

I look up and see Susan emerge from the shower. She's got a towel wrapped around her head and dressing gown on.

'Susan, you need to get ready quick. We need to go find someone.'

Susan nods, grabs some clothing and disappears back inside the bathroom. Fifteen minutes later, we're in the car and on our way to drop Maggie back. I take her across in the tender to Craigantlet and bring the little boat back. The first stop after that is the house of McAvoy. On the way I think of some ruse to say to his wife if she answers the door, instead.

Knocking on the door, I see the woman from a few nights ago answer it. Looking haggard and down, her hairs crumpled, and she's standing there in blue jeans and a tee shirt, a number of kids running around behind her.

'What?' she says. 'How can help you?' Her tone is curt and she says she has better things to do.

'I was just looking for your husband, Mr. McAvoy,' I say. 'He asked me to do some business and he hasn't turned up. It is urgent and I need to speak to him. I'm from the local council.'

She stares at me intently and turns away before turning back to me.

'He's not here,' she says. 'He went out.'

'Oh, okay' I say. 'Do you know where I might be able to catch up with him?'

The tears are starting to well in her eyes. She's beginning to shake as one of her children runs up to her leg but she fends the child off in a way that doesn't appear reminiscent of a doting mother.

'He's been gone since last night,' she says. Her voice begins to shake. 'He said he'd be back. He said he'd be here.'

The man is definitely missing and I reckon I have to move quickly. It's time to drop the disguise. I need to find out from this woman everything she knows.

'Look, Mrs. McAvoy, you need to understand, I've been following your husband for the last number of days. He's mixed up in something where he disappears off to the Fairy Pools and he's given tasks to do at this druidic meeting. But it's not what it seems, and I think he's been taken somewhere against his will. My name's Paddy Smythe and I'm a private investigator, and I need to know anything about where he's gone. Anything he said to you.'

'I don't know anything,' she says. 'I don't know.'

'Have you got a room he uses as an office? I need to check his diary.'

The woman is in a flap and a panic. I feel she's just reaching out to me now because she doesn't know what else to do. She grabs me and takes me through the house into the office, which seems ludicrous because I could be anyone. She doesn't ask for any identification or anything. But I guess she's beyond her wits end. Despite his always abusive nature to her, she clearly has concerns for him.

At the office, I start to search through a large wooden bureau. There is lots of information about the farm, but I'm looking for something different, something you wouldn't keep in the same way. I start to open drawers and one of them's locked.

'That's a special one,' she says. 'I haven't seen inside that.'

I pull on it, but it's not coming away.

'He must have a key,' she says. 'Maybe he carries it on him, I've never seen it. He hit me when I tried to clean that once.'

With that, she drops to her knees, beginning to cry. I know I should go over and help her. I know I should actually comfort her, but frankly, I haven't got the time at the moment. So instead, I step to the door, call out to Susan, who comes running with a crowbar from the car.

A jab made into the door soon breaks it open and I begin to pull out the contents. Mrs. McAvoy is still on the floor crying, and even when Susan comes in, she looks up without any sort of shock, almost assuming this is normal. I start to spread the contents on the floor of which there are a number of photographs. They have fallen out of a small black book. The photographs seem to be a number of different men and women, and then I recognize one person he threatened the other day. There are three photographs of Anna. It seems that James had quite a crush on her. No wonder he wanted to threaten her to the point of making her do something to pleasure him. There's also times and dates. Maybe they'll be able to match up with beatings and other threatening behavior within the local area.

The man is no seasoned criminal. He's kept a record of everything. As I'm flicking through the book, Susan's going through a small packet of photographs. Unlike the other ones, they've not been sent to him; maybe he's taken them himself because they're only six by four photographs, much smaller. Whilst they are all of women, a large number of them are of Jenny Carnegie.

'Hey, Paddy, look at these,' says Susan.

She hands me the photographs. I choke at the site of the first one, Jenny Carnegie in an image that leaves little to even a doctor's imagination. Maybe that's how she drew him in, using her body. Which for James McAvoy doesn't seem unreasonable because the man seems to be reacting to every woman around. Jenny, obviously is a weak spot, enticed him, seduced him, and then brought him into the ring. Now, he's in so tight he can't get out. It makes me wonder if there is a decent family man hidden away, deep down. It's a rather nice platitude.

Sometimes you use something to try and make you feel less bad about the people you're looking at, trying to make you think of them more as human than as the destructive monsters they turn into. I'm having a very hard time doing that with Jenny Carnegie at the moment; she seems to just be breaking everything. It makes me wonder if Simon Haldon, the landowner she's sleeping with, knows what he's getting into. Is he being used by her? But then again, what's his connection? Maybe he's got the money. He's got room to be able to hide it and move it on.

'Shall I package it all up,' Susan says.

'Everything—it's all evidence. We can take it to the police.'

The woman's head flies up. 'What do you mean, the police? What's happened to him? What's he involved with?' And she reaches over grabbing the photographs off Susan. I see her face as she looks down. Jenny Carnegie's in the top photograph in a rather revealing way.

'Who's this?' she screams. 'Who's this? Has he been sleeping with this woman? Has he been messing around? I knew he'd been messing around; I knew. Where is he? I'll kill the bastard.'

'No, you won't,' I say. 'You'll sit here, and you'll keep quiet. I'll deal with this. I'll get to the police; he's in over his head, and this is nothing. The woman you're looking at, it's nothing compared to the danger he's in. Trust me, stay calm, stay quiet.

I'm going to find your husband now. If I haven't come back to you by first thing tomorrow, call the police.'

As we leave the house, I'm unsure what the woman will do, maybe she'll call this in earlier. But I hope not. I think she still cares for him, whatever she thinks has been done with him. She stuck with him after I saw him strike her. Maybe there's something, maybe some form of control. I don't know. I haven't got time to work that relationship out. I need to get moving and find our man.

'We'll see if we can find his car, see if he's around the area from last night. We'll also go to Portree and look around the area where he picked up the hoods,' I say to Susan. 'Then if we can't find them, I'm bringing Jenny off the boat. I'm going to bring her into the police with all the evidence. But call Hans. Even if I hand her to the police, I want more evidence. I think we can get it from that landowner. And tell Hans it's a quick job; I need him here now, from wherever he is. I want to infiltrate tonight.

Susan nods, picking up her phone and disappearing. I get into the car and then turn back and look at the house. Mrs McAvoy's looking from the door at me, tears streaming from her face. And part of me wishes I had more people, someone to leave here with her, because really the police should be involved at this point. But I need to get Jenny back ashore, in case she cries kidnap. The only people that have seen where I've had her on the boat are my people. And that's the way I'm going to keep it.

But I also stop to think while Susan's making the call. They made James McAvoy plan the whole thing. He was contacting the hoods and then they burnt down somewhere completely different. They murdered two people. And it dawns on me

145

he's been set up. And I've been set up. I was hired to find their mole. They knew something was up. They knew somebody wanted out or something like that. The fact I was brought in, then rescued her so I would feel obliged to find out what was going on. I find him and when I put pressure on, he talks to me and he caves in.

For some reason, they doubted him. When I came in, he went for it. Maybe it's a test, but why such a test—there's something about it. The operation was at risk, whatever the whole operation actually is. Extorting money on that level, it's going somewhere, it's moving somewhere. Come on, Paddy, think.

I realise I need to see inside the landowner's house, to break in and find out if the money is there, if he's the one transferring it. It'll give Martha a chance to follow the trail properly. But I also want that woman off the boat and into police custody before she can phone anyone else. Before she gets people to come and take her off the boat. Martha's good, but they'll outnumber her. Who knows what would happen?

Twenty minutes later in the car back in Portree, we drive around the winding streets looking for any sign of McAvoy's car. But there's none. James McAvoy's vehicle doesn't appear to be about. Even as we check where we were before, there's nothing, no sign of the car or any hoods. If they clocked us last night, they'll probably go to ground for a couple of days at least.

So, after an hour spinning around, I take Susan back to her hotel. I tell her to phone Martha, prep her I'm coming, because I want Jenny straight off the boat. And Martha gives her to nobody but me. And I need Martha ready for picking up files tonight from Hans. I know Maggie will complain but she is to be told in no uncertain terms that she is remaining on the boat.

And with that, I make a call outside in the car before I depart Susan's hotel. It's a confidential line to the police and I don't give my name. But I tell them I've got information, that I need to meet somebody about last night's fire. I give them a place where I'll be, which is just outside Portree at a small car park that leads to the forest. One of the joys of Scotland, so many little trails and passes, that there's always a handy tourist car park. I don't give my name. I don't give my number and the call is from a mobile SIM card for once and one time only.

It's late evening when I get into the tender. I make my way across to the Craigantlet where Martha is standing on deck with Jenny. Martha only gives me a nod as Jenny gets down into the boat and I tell her to keep quiet as we head to the other side.

She asked where we're going, and again I tell her to be quiet, saying that there are people looking for her and we need to keep on the move. I don't know what she's thinking because surely, she must know I'm looking at dropping her in to the police. Maybe she understands I've worked out her plans. But I keep the pretence up and say nothing on the other side. We get into the car and I start to drive. There's only one place I'm going. That car park for my rendezvous with the police.

Chapter Eighteen

J enny Carnegie is nervous in the car, which is something I've not really seen from her. Her left hand is beginning to shake. And she keeps glancing towards me, her hand moving across to my knee.

'Paddy, I'm scared. 'If they're coming after me, I'm scared. Where are we going? Are we going to hole up somewhere? You and I can just hole up out of the way for a couple of days, be away from them, just you and me,' she says.

I note some of the confidence has come back in her voice and she leans over, one hand moving up on her blouse, putting her hand down between her neck and her chest. I know what she's trying to do. She knows how to get me to look at her and she's doing it with practiced ease. But the good thing about driving is there's a road out there and I keep my eyes firmly on it. Well, half on it. I just want to make sure she doesn't make any sudden movements either. The woman is a cold-blooded killer. She at least orders the death of others, so I need to be careful.

She has her hand on my thigh, moving it up and down, stroking it. And she's starting some tears now, telling me, almost begging me to take her away and look after her for a few days. She's even running the idea that she will somehow make it worth my while. It's very crass, though, even if she does it in a very smooth way. But the idea that someone investigating something, I'll just happily disappear off for a couple of days of fun while there's danger all around me and other people are in trouble, baffles me.

But obviously, she's manipulated many men before, so maybe I'm misjudging her. Maybe she's got this right and I don't know. But she just hasn't got me right.

The sun's low but the day is still warm when we pull into the car park. Long shadows are running off the trees. It's not that well-known path and certainly it's barely marked on the maps. There's one other car here, but no one in it. I'm about five minutes early for my meeting with the police. I want to have scouted the place before their arrival.

I get out of the car, to wait, and Jenny watches me through the windscreen. She sees that I'm looking for something. After a couple of minutes, she steps out and I tell her to get back in the car, but she ignores me. Since my senses are on edge, maybe she knows what I'm going to do. She steps up before me and says.

'I haven't been entirely truthful with you, Paddy, have I?' I give her a cold stare. 'But you did me a great favour. You outed him. He could have brought us all down. I started to notice it when he talked to the newspaper. But you've done a great job. How about fifty grand to just go away. I'd even throw a little extra on top of that?'

She starts to undo her blouse to the point where I can see her chest and underwear underneath.

'I don't mind what your fancy is.' she says. 'But this is fifty grand. And you still have a good job and be a lot happier and a lot richer. You know it makes sense, Paddy? You can take the money and entertain the little trollop on your boat. She's not really much for you, is she? I'm sure you prefer something like this.'

Now the blouse is coming off the shoulders, so I shake my head.

'Get back in the car.' I say, but she continues to walk forward and there's a hand up on my shoulder.

'I've never done it with someone who . . .' and she looks at where my arm isn't. 'Does it make a difference to you?' she says.

She is going for my weakness. She's looking to try and make me feel guilt or for what I'm missing, trying to bring back possibly the time when it happened. If she's doing that, she hasn't a hope. That moment sticks in my mind every day, every morning, when I wake up. It particularly comes on those days when I can feel the arm, even though it's not there. Her hand's down my chest and I see where she's making for. I brush her off but she pushes again towards me, her hand going down and then with a sudden grasp, she squeezes tight between my legs.

I could say I just brushed off this incident, but bloody hell it was invasive. Almost instinctively, I swing a slap across her face, not something gentle, something hard, so it sends her reeling back against the car, as I bend over double still feeling the pain from where she grabbed me, her long nails having dug in. She jumps at me hands around my throat. Not as tall as me, and with both hands on the throat, it's easy to throw a punch into her stomach. It's thrown as hard as I would to any man and she collapses on the ground, struggling to breathe, the wind completely knocked out of her.

I pick her up by hair, push up her against the car, and then push myself up against her backside to hold her there. With her blouse off her shoulders, it's difficult for her arms to move about. I reach into my back pocket, pulling out a small set of cuffs, clicking them on the first arm and then dragging that arm across to the other. It's not easy when you've only got one hand. I've got a hold on the empty cuff, dragging the cuffed arm across to try to put it onto the other arm but she's flailing it about. It takes me a minute, but I see the empty cuff snapped them on. At this point, I lift up her blouse, pushing it back over her shoulders. Marching around to the other side of the car, I push up her against the car again, holding her with my weight while I open the door to the front passenger seat and then throw her inside.

She glares at me and I can see the anger. It's amazing how her eyes change from the leering look one moment, as if she's ready to take me to whatever heaven I want, and the next moment, she's looking to kill me.

She doesn't kill people, I think to myself, the way she came after me. She has no idea how to do it. That's why she gets other people involved. She must be the master planner to this, running everyone else.

With her inside the car, I stand at the rear of it, watching for anyone else who arrives. I'm not going anywhere until the cops get here. Then at least there will be two of us, and we'd be able to drive her somewhere easy enough with my single arm. I don't fancy trying to drive a car and hold her in place. Maybe I should have brought a gun, but when the police are involved, someone standing with a gun doesn't always look good, especially if it's unregistered. Which, of course, mine is, just in case I ever have to use it. The last thing I want is them knowing I have a gun.

It's about ten minutes later when a dark car drives in. I see from the sticker on it, it's a rental car from a local firm, the same one we've been using, I think I can see one person in it. Having parked, a large man climbs out. He's wearing a hoodie, which must be a triple x size because he fills it like some sort of American wrestler. I can't see the face as it's held down. He comes forward and it's only when he starts to get close that I start to panic.

'You asked to meet the police, sir, confidentially,' says a voice. And then the hoodie comes back and I see the face of Sergeant Gillespie. I cycle around the car, keeping him on the other side of it from me. 'Looks like you have my boss,' he says. 'You don't want to cage her up. She doesn't like men handling her like that.' I watch him leering through the window.

'Is that how she got you into this as well?' I say, as I watch the man enjoy the view. 'Couldn't keep it in your pants.'

He snaps his view back to me. 'You did a good job, Mr. Smythe. They said you were good, came highly recommended. It was hard trying to work out who was speaking. We'd had a few confidential phone calls about the beatings, someone who felt guilty, but who would hang up. We couldn't have that, could we. And it was good of you to use that confidential line. Good of me to intercept it. Stroke of luck that.

'Did you enjoy the fire?' He says, almost laughing. 'We wrote the note to him, nicely sending you right to the place we set out for him. But then you were quick enough to get to the other fire, quick enough to get inside, but not quick enough to save them, Mr. Smythe. And not quick enough to save yourself this time. They won't find you either. I can't leave a one arm body, too easy. And once I'm done with you, I'll get rid of that boat as well.'

He's talking a lot, and I want him to because I'm trying to

152

work out how I'm going to get out of here. He's a big brute. I'm not sure if I'll be able to take him on. Also, I've got no way of keeping him down as my handcuffs are on Jenny Carnegie, in the front seat. He may even get her to help him. Although, I doubt it, he's probably enjoying the position she's in at the moment. Looking forward to a grateful boss once he's disposed of me.

I fully believe that Jenny can pay in kind like that. I'm really falling out of favour with this woman fast. It's like my mother always used to say, 'Be careful what a tin looks like, the contents might be off.'

He makes a run for me on one side of the car and I circle before he comes back the other way. At some point, I have to run but I think he might be quicker than me. Then he forces my hand because he jumps up upon to the bonnet of the car, then up onto the roof of it, so he's looking down at me.

'How do you fight with one arm?' he asks. 'Apparently, you gave our hoodlums a bit of a thrashing. I've always said the trouble with young people these days is they don't know how to fight. Not old school like you or me, Mr. Smythe. But fighting with one arm, that's impressive.'

And then he jumps down so he's close to me. He makes the mistake of running towards me fast and I step to one side and launch a kick up by his jaw, catching him, sending him spinning against the car. But he rights himself quickly. Damn that was a good kick to the head. A lot of people would hit the floor with that.

'Oh, like that, Mr. Smythe, is it?' he says. 'I'll need to be more cautious with you.'

This time he takes a different stance. I'm not sure what it is but it is karate based. However, I'm really struggling, but either way, it's pretty irrelevant because he's coming to me and I need to get ready. He throws a fist that I block with my arm, but the other fist comes fast, and I have to duck away. But it's a feint, and he catches me with a kick to my left midriff, sending me sprawling to the floor.

He's fast and jumps on top of me. I work hard to get my arm in the way as he rains punches at my head. A few glance off the back of it but my heads rings. He reaches down with both hands but that's a mistake. I butt my head up at his face, smashing my forehead into it. Bloods spurts out. As he reaches up for his nose with both hands, I roll with all my might causing him to turn over as well. Now he's on his back and I could try to follow up, but I've got one arm and I can't get myself balanced. So, I roll away, rising up onto my feet, as he stands up, his hand on his nose, cursing me.

'Did she offer you some? The boss?' he says. 'Did she offer you something? You should have taken it, a little enjoyment before you die. She would have killed you while you were doing it. You could have gone happy. Now, you're going to go miserable because I'm going to make you feel every bit of this.'

Again, he comes forward, and I strike him with a kick to the face. But I don't catch him as well as last time. He is able to grab my leg, turning it, twisting it hard. I fall to the ground but when he comes down behind me, I kick out with the other foot, catching him on the face. His hand releases, and I roll away as quick as I can, coming to my feet.

But as I stand up, he hits me with a rugby tackle, and we fall to the floor again. He manages to get two really hard blows on my face and I'm feeling groggy as he pins me down. But his leg position is wrong. He's left himself open and I drive a knee hard, right up in between his groin. He screams, especially as I drive another three times right up in there.

I turn and see her face in the car. She's smiling at me, almost laughing. But I can't hang about, so I turn and run. Heading out to the main road, I hear him get up, hear her shouting for him to follow me. It's about half a mile out to the main road and I scarper with everything I've got. I'm not that steady on my feet, swaying from side to side across the road.

Behind me, I hear shouting, but he can't be running well. I really wouldn't fancy dealing with the bruises he's going to be having. As I reach the main road, I just pray to God that somebody's there. Because he's stopped following me, I'm sure he'll be in the car.

I see the bus come along, so stick out my hand, waving it. That's the good thing about this sort of area, the bus driver slows down and I jump on board. Pulling out my wallet and holding it with my teeth, I manage to throw some coins out to him.

'Are you all right son?' he says. 'You look like you've had a bit of a rough time.'

'It's all right,' I say. 'Had a bit of a fall, cut my face bad. Just take me to Portree. I'll walk up to the hospital.

'That's a wee bit out of my way' he says, 'but I'll take you there. No charge—just go sit down.'

I thank him, trying to stay as low as I possibly can inside the bus. There's another three people on it and I get about twenty minutes before I arrive at the hospital. I step out and thank him and he asks me if 'I need help getting inside.' I shake my head and off he drives.

As soon as he's gone, I run into the undergrowth in case I've been followed. I take out my mobile and give Susan a call, telling her to get to the hospital car park. She's not to get out of the car—I'll get in. And with that, I sit down on my bottom looking out through the hedges. Thankfully, nobody's tailed me. Damn it, Paddy, you should have seen that one coming.

Chapter Nineteen

I place a call to Martha telling her to get Maggie, to weigh anchor, and get Craigantlet on the move, somewhere away from here. It's always a risk that they could go for them, although in fairness, I wouldn't take Martha on, not when she's on a boat and can see you coming. I tell Martha about the woman's attempt to kill me, followed by the police officer's.

My next call is to see where Hans is because I want to get to Simon Hilden's. There's too much going on at the moment and I want some concrete proof to hand over about where this money's going from where it is. If you can trace the money, you can always show the evidence and get a proper case because it'll be a hard task trying to convince people to talk against them. Now Hans is someone who can get me inside places and who can also get inside technology.

When Susan picks me up, there's shake of a head because I must look a bit of a mess. But we continue to our rendezvous, just outside Portree, with Hans. His look at me is a little less critical and he tells me he has all the equipment ready. Given the way circumstances are moving, I tell Susan she's got to sit and be the getaway driver for us, while Hans comes in with me. We put Martha up on a link, so anything we find can be sent directly to her.

'But what if we don't find any money?' says Susan. 'What if we can't trace it? What have we got?'

'Apart from them trying to beat me up, only what people say against them. It's going to be hard to link it back to Jenny Carnegie,' I say, 'but we also need to move quick; otherwise, McAvoy will be dead. As much as I don't care for the man, the last thing we need are more dead bodies—we've already had two.'

It's approximately eleven o'clock when we get to the landowner's house. Unlike previous places I've broken into, Simon Hilden doesn't have a lot of security here, no guards patrolling, nobody wandering around. It's pretty much just his own house and I wonder if that's a front.

Hans scans the building and says we go in by one of the doors at the rear. The building's large and there's several lights on, some on the stairwell, a large one that leads up through the centre of the house. From what I remember there's office space at the top and bedrooms.

Having donned our black gear, Hans and I make our way round to the rear of the building while Susan sits out front in the car. She pulls away into a small lane further up the road, one of those ones that has a picnic area for families during the summer, but now it's providing a good hideout for her.

The house is quiet and I'm not sure if there are any servants anyway, but if they have any, they've all been sent away. There were none lurking last time. Stepping through the rear door, I can't hear anything and so together with Hans, we make our way through the bottom floor. We find kitchens, sitting rooms, and a game room, nothing that really holds our interest. So, we gently start to climb up to the first floor.

There are some shower rooms, guest quarters, what looks

like some smaller office spaces and some computers which Hans switches on and starts to make explorations into. He touches equipment here and there and I have no idea how he does it or what he's doing but I hear him whispering quietly into his microphone, telling Martha he's sending something.

It's then I hear something upstairs, physical groans and grunts. I've been a private investigator too long to not know what those sighs mean—two people enjoying themselves. I point at the equipment, telling Hans to keep going on with what he's doing, while I make my way up the flight of stairs to the top floor. I scour on the corridor but can soon tell the room the action's taking place in. I walk beyond it, step into another room which is a bedroom neatly laid out but which looks like it hasn't been touched in a while. Maybe it's a guest quarter, for a special guest, because there's an intertwining door.

I make my way over to the wall and listen in. After about five minutes, there's a quieter time, shall we say, and I hear him start to stroll about. I guess there's an en suite inside the main bedroom because I hear a shower going and after a while, I hear someone rubbing themselves down with a towel.

'Shall we move somewhere more comfortable,' says a man's voice, and then I hear Jenny Carnegie agree. I race back to the door of the bedroom I am in, to see them walk from their own bedroom, down the corridor to the far end of the house. It's Simon Hilden with her, which is not surprising, this being his house, and they're both clothed in dressing gowns, sumptuous white affairs, like something you'd wrap up on a winter's night. I watch them get to the far end of the landing before turning to what looks like the outside wall of the house and I realize they're stepping out unto a balcony. I follow along the corridor quickly, keeping myself low, before peering out through a window to see them standing, Jenny holding onto the balcony and Simon holding on to her from behind.

'You need to move the money, Simon,' she says. 'We may need to get out quick. Can you move the cash quickly?'

'It's all put aside,' he replies, 'but I'll do it tonight and put it in the other place, nice and safe and I'll sail myself once we move to the yacht. It'll be a pity to leave this all behind though. It wasn't bad for a couple of years.'

'I'll have the loose ends tied up by tonight,' Jenny says. 'I'll implicate them all in it. We'll bring him, make them all do it, then I'll get out. I'll be gone but they'll think I'm dead. The girl's a remarkable likeness.'

'I've always liked the way you just get things done,' he says, and his hands start to roam over her. There's no fight in Jenny Carnegie; she seems to be enjoying this and I wonder if this is the man she wants. Usually she's playing them along but she's not even making the effort here. It's like they actually genuinely both want each other.

'What about Smythe?' the man says.

'What about him? He has no firm evidence; he has nothing he can really take to the police. And I'll be dead. He knows nothing about you and me, no one does, no one's been here, no one's seen my little money deposits. We've put nothing through any banks. All we need to do is get on the boat and then we'll put it into an account, slowly.

'We need to be going anyway. I need to make sure things are organized and that they happen. One more dance around the Pools, and then we're gone. I'll see you at the yacht about five in the morning, just you and me,' she says.

'I'll miss this though,' Hilden says.

'There are other places to see, nicer places. Places where

we'll be warm in the sun.

'I meant up here. Two years, two years in the middle of the night, I think there's time for one more.'

I can guess what's coming, and as I peer up over the window, it's confirmed as dressing gowns fall. It's a perfect time to get on the move out of here and I make my way along the corridor, back down the stairs and find Hans. He tells me he's transferred a lot of stuff, but Martha can't see anything, most stuff seems to be pretty mundane. I tell him to continue for the moment, but to hurry as our targets could be on the move soon.

I explain to Hans they're planning to move their money tonight, but we haven't found out where it is. He suggests we go outside and look for the car, put a tracker on it and when I ask if he has one on him, he delves into the small bag he carries over his shoulder and pulls out a device that looks so tiny. I nod and we make our way to the stairwell before exiting again by the rear door.

Hans moves over to the cars and places a tracker under a large Land Rover, sitting outside. At one point as I watch the house, lights start to come on, as the couple descend the stairs but he's able to fit in a tracker onto Jenny Carnegie's car as well. We retire to the shadows of the bushes surrounding the house and watch as Simon Hilden and Jenny Carnegie pack his car. I notice five briefcases come out and I guess that's the cash. They go into the boot of the Land Rover covered by a number of travel cases. Together the pair turn round and look at the house and he puts his arm around her, once again. She's dressed in a tracksuit now, just grey sweats because I guess she's going to be performing her dance. He's in casual jeans and a jumper.

They stand there for what must be ten to fifteen minutes,

looking at the house. It's bizarre, the woman's off to tie up loose ends which I presume is to dispose of people but she's looking at this house as if she's simply moving and saying a fond farewell to a happy home. Jenny then turns and together they embrace, and I hear the whisper of, 'See you in about four hours.' With that they step into their separate cars and I look questioningly at Hans. He tells me that his tracker's working.

As the headlights come on and the two cars depart, Hans and I run back to the road. I find Susan in the car, tell her to head for the Fairy Pools straight away and pick up my mobile. I need to ring into the station, but then I have a second thought. Instead I ring in and ask for Martin Kerr, the police officer I spoke to previously. He's not there, but at home instead so instead I ring a different number.

Given that it's past midnight, most people will be asleep, and I get a rather disorientated woman answering the phone. When I ask for Detective Inspector Macleod, she asks if that's Paddy and I say hello to Jane. She then shouts for Seoras.

'Yes, this is Macleod.'

'Macleod, Smythe. I need your help and I need it quick. I've got something going down at the Fairy Pools in Skye. I believe that somebody could be about to kill someone. I've also got a car disappearing with several million, I guess, in cash closing off the back end of a scam that involves extortion here on the isle. I need to get through to good people in the Skye police office, but there's also a bad egg in there. So, I need you to get hold of Martin Kerr and you can give him my name. Tell him I need assistance as quick as he can. They won't give me his number phoning into the office and I don't have it.'

'Wait,' says Macleod, 'just give me that again; who's about to die?'

'Look, Macleod, I haven't got time on this one. You've trusted me before. I've come through. You need to just call and tell them I need a large police presence down to the Fairy Pools. Quick as possible. Can you do that for me? We also have a tracker running on the car with several million inside that comes from extortion. I don't have time to explain—I'm on the way now to the Fairy Pools to try and stop it.'

'Don't do anything,' he says. 'Wait until they get there. I'll get on the phone and get things moving.'

'People could be dead by then, I'm going in and I'm going to stop it,' I say, 'but you need to get this done for me; can you do that?'

'Okay, Smythe, but for goodness sake, why this time of the morning?'

'I haven't time,' I say and cancel the call. Macleod will come through for me. I know that, but I don't know if it'll happen in time. It's amazing how long things take to get moving, especially when there's been no evidence of foul play beforehand. Susan's got the car going in full throttle, with Hans in the rear and he asks me if we need to pack weapons?

'No, don't, because it just gets messy if they turn up and we're standing there with weapons pointed at people. Especially you with your background.'

He gives me a smile with that and I direct Susan to the car park we were in before. There's a number of cars there already and I see the one that Jenny Carnegie pulled away in from her lover's house. But there's also a van there this time that I've never seen before and it makes me think of the thugs. There could be significant numbers here so I hope the police bring significant numbers with them.

We park our car and together stride along the path quickly,

trying to find where this dance is taking place. I check the previous spot, where I last saw Jenny Carnegie getting changed for her to dance, and sure enough, there's a set of clothes there but they're not hers. She's in sweatpants; these are a pair of pyjamas, women's pyjamas, and I think about what she said. She really has gone and got someone else. She's going to make it look like she died by putting someone else in her place.

'We need to hurry,' I say, 'because someone's going to die and I don't even know who it is.'

Chapter Twenty

We're following the track down to the Fairy Pools, the one we followed before, and we see the men at their druidic performance, a strange mass with much more deadly intent. It's awkward because we need to sneak up on them and yet I don't want to take too long because there are lives at threat, including an innocent woman whose name I don't even know yet. As we push along the path and through another clearing, we come out beside the Fairy Pool that they usually use but I see no one. Peering through the twilight darkness, I hear nothing.

'Is this the right place?' asks Hans. 'There's no one here.'

I can see Susan panicking. 'This is it, Paddy. We were here last time; this is where we watched them from over there behind that rock—we're in the right place.'

'Then they're going somewhere different,' says Hans, always one for the completely obvious statement.

'Quiet,' I say, 'everyone, just stay quiet.' There's a light breeze blowing, and I can hear a faint rustle, small vegetation moving back and forward. There's a faint noise then I can hear a low droning. I point up away from me and Hans nods.

The three of us sprint along a new track, one we haven't been along before, that heads up the side of the river. The track's fairly weak, not easy to follow, especially in this light, but it is not there for the tourists. And that makes a lot of sense if they intend to dispatch someone tonight.

It isn't long before we can see a clearing up ahead, right beside one of the pools. There's a gathering of men, all dressed in white and there in the middle is Jenny Carnegie. She's dancing, spinning around in her dress of veils, the one she wore the first time we saw her. Slowly, she reaches forward, whispering into each of the man's ears. We get up close, trying to stay hidden but also trying to overhear what's happening.

'There's one less,' says Susan. 'One less! They must have him somewhere else; maybe they don't have him here.'

'It's because he's not part of the group anymore,' I whisper, 'they're going to finish him off.'

I watch closely and Jenny disappears from sight, gliding along a small track and then behind a hillock, before someone comes out dressed with antler horns on his head. He has a large gown, like the rest of the men but looks different, almost like he's in charge. In front of him is James McAvoy wearing the garb he normally would to these meetings, and in front of him is a woman in the same dress worn by Jenny Carnegie. But if you look closely, she's not the same height. Her mouth is gagged, hands tied behind her back and James McAvoy is dragging her forward. It's then I see the outline of the gun in the hand of the man with the antlers on his head but I note his face is masked.

I don't know what Jenny said to the men, but they seem eager to gather around her or who they think is her. The woman is struggling and is tied to a post beside one of the Fairy Pools. The men form a circle around her or at least a half circle. There's a rushing behind her, a drop where the water can be heard tumbling into the pool below. The river runs beside this place and as the moon deems to shine, it lights up the pools giving an eerie glow back off them. There's enough light to see clear shapes, if not detail, and I watch the man with antlers hand a knife to James McAvoy.

'Susan,' I say, 'go run behind us; run to where that hillock they came out from is. Go and watch who's there. Be careful, give yourself enough distance because I think Jenny Carnegie is going to be there and I reckon she's going to start running.'

Hans taps me on the shoulder as I'm speaking to Susan. He points and I see James McAvoy with his knife raised, standing before the woman. There's a chant going up, all the men participating, and the woman's thrashing but is still bound to the post. The sound gets louder and louder but, in the background, I can hear sirens coming. It looks like Macleod managed to get through, but I don't know how far away they are.

James McAvoy puts down the knife and finds a gun put to the back of his neck. He's clearly been told to kill the woman. The man with the antlers on his head says something, and it must have been good because James McAvoy picks up his knife again with a renewed determination, steps forward and looks ready to slit the woman's throat.

I tap Hans on the shoulder, and he nods, sprinting forward from our hiding place. We are only thirty feet away, and most of the men have their backs to us. By the time the first ones on the far side have us in their sights and realize what's happening, to start pointing, the others are only turning around. Hans clatters into several of them. They tumble to the ground and he's carved a path for me. I run past, clattering into James McAvoy, causing him to drop his knife and stumble. I see him pitch over the edge of the small cliff, descending down into the

167

pool. It can only be a twenty-foot drop, so he'll be all right.

As I start to recover myself, I turn round to protect the girl and see the man with the antlers raise a knife. Hans is on the floor scrapping with many of the men jumping around him and more come towards me. The man with the knife swings at the girl and I manage to get my arm up, stifling his attack slightly but he slashes her across the arm.

She tries to scream but it's muffled by the gag in her mouth and the man with the antlers steps forward again, arm raised. I turn round, try to throw a punch but he swings his arm right at me, blocking it and so I kick him in the knees. He begins to tumble, and I feel somebody grab my leg. I kick hard behind me and realize I'm about to be overwhelmed with all these men in the fight. Hans is suffering the same fate. So, with one shoulder, I hit the woman tied to the post in the midriff, causing the post to lift out of the ground. With my right arm I swing round, catch hold of the legs of the man with the antlers, causing him to twist and all three of us drop off the cliff edge into the pool below.

There's a crash water of water around me and I submerge. Kicking hard with my legs, I get back to the surface and scan desperately to find the woman. She's attached to a post and if she's facing the wrong way, she won't be able to breathe.

There's a strong flow of water into the pool at the moment and I feel myself starting to get carried down the stream. But I also see the legs of the woman and reach over and manage to grab the wooden post. She's face down, so desperately, I grab her, rotating her round. Beside me, there's a pair of antlers.

Now I have my arm free, I throw a punch towards them but they don't move, casually drifting down ahead of me. It's only then I feel something behind me, and I turn to see the face of Sergeant Gillespie. The man's still holding a knife and he brings it down, forcing me to twist as it stabs through the water. He tries to come back again but his arm strength is taken from trying to lift the knife back out of the water; his attempt to stab is weak and I push off, letting the woman sail away from me, still attached to the post.

I feel another thrust come towards me. This time it connects but again the effect is dulled due to the water the knife has to go through before it reaches me. However, I can still feel the bite in my shoulder. I allow myself to sink, reach round with my legs, tying them around Gillespie before I reach forward with my hand, grabbing his wrist of the hand holding the knife. We emerge up to the surface briefly. He grins at me, his left arm reaching out for my neck. He's so close, I just react instinctively and butt him, right between the eyes. It catches him unawares for a second time in twenty-four hours. For a moment he sinks and starts to scrabble with his legs and I break away to swim off. But I misjudge it.

He's not been compromised as much as I thought and a hand grabs my ankle, before I feel the knife again, cutting across the back of my calf. There's a shooting pain going through me, and I'm trying not to think about that but instead to concentrate on getting away, If I could get out of the water, it would be an easier fight for me. But I bring my left leg down through the water as hard as I can and connect with his face. It's a good blow and gives me a moment to swim away. But I can hear the splashes of him after me each time I come up for air.

Soon we drift into some rocks and clambering out of the water, I see the woman is stuck, the post having wedged between a couple of rocks. Her mouth's out of the water, even if she's freaking out, desperately struggling. I scan the water for signs of Gillespie. and see him emerging, standing upright, all six feet four of him. With both arms wide, he comes at me, swinging several times with the knife. Behind me is more water and a difficult surface to climb up and get away. I'm going to have to stand and fight.

He moves in and I wait for him to stab. If I'm fortunate, he'll jab on my right side and I can grab his knife arm with my hand. But he doesn't, and goes to my left. I shimmy right, bring a leg up and kick him in the midriff, simply knocking him back a foot. He then steps forward again, but this time swings wildly, from my left to my right and I step back allowing the blade to pass before following it with my hand and grabbing his wrist.

Now I've turned him sideways, I'm able to kick up, right up to the back of his head. It's hard and brutal, and it's meant to be, causing him to stumble forward. I still have his arm in my hand and I yank it sharply causing him to cry out; the knife falls and as I pull him back towards me, I use my other leg to kick up into his face. I swear there's a crack of his jaw or there's at least his teeth meeting each other quickly. He falls to the ground, his face splashing in the water.

Keeping an eye on him, I grab the post the woman's attached to, dragging her up to the side. When she's out and clear, I tried to undo the knots, but I can't. Her eyes are wide, panicking, looking at me as if I'm the enemy. But I also see the blue lights in the distance, and I hear the cries of 'Police!'

'You're going to be alright, love,' I say. 'You're all right; he's out cold. The police are here; they'll free you.' I look at her shivering in the cold. It might be the middle of summer, but she's been immersed and the outfit they made her wear wasn't much to begin with. Hans appears beside me, jumping down from the bank above, telling me that Susan's called, and Jenny's making a run for it.

Hans reaches down as I throw my single arm up, and he pulls me up to the top of the bank. His face is cut and he's bloody. We don't want to get held up so as we see the police arrive, we avoid them, moving back to the far side of the bank, conveniently moving around them. They seem to be coming from a different direction anyway and I'm not sure if they used the same car park as we have. As we get back to the car park, believing that Jenny will have fled from there in her car, I can see our own car and Susan at the wheel.

Jenny's up ahead. I can see the lights of her car come on and as she starts to drive, Susan doesn't hesitate and simply floors the pedal, cutting off Jenny's escape route. Neither woman gives way and both cars collide into each other. There are airbags going off and a sickening crunch and I can hear windscreens breaking. I slosh along, still soaked through from having landed in the river, and see the car catch on fire.

As we get close, I tell Hans to grab Susan and get her clear. Before me I see fuel running out of the tank. I pull open the door of Jenny's car and she seems to be unconscious. I reach across, undo her belt and try to pull her out. A hand reaches round and grabs my throat.

'You should have died, Mr. Smythe,' she says. 'I'll make sure you do now. '

I see the hand holding what looks like a small dagger and desperately try to step away. It misses my neck but ends up lodged in my shoulder and again a hot pain races down my side. My head's down at her chest, from reaching across with a belt. I can't think of anything else to do except lift it quickly and catch her under her chin with the back of my head. It makes me cry out in pain but it has the desired effect, causing her hands to fall off me.

I spin away, telling her she has to get out, before the car explodes. There's a flame and I see the ignition of the fuel. There's an instinct making me reach forward to drag her out, but a bigger hand grabs me from behind and pulls me down to the ground. There's a large explosion and I feel hot fire passing over me. And then there's just immense heat and a hand pulling me clear, dragging me. I hear a scream. Looking up, I can see the figure of Jenny Carnegie. It's barely moving, but I can't get near that car because of the heat.

Beside me, Susan screams until Hans takes her in his arms and holds her tight, telling her not to look. There's a smell in the air that I recognize and it's one the police officers would have had at the hotel that burned the previous night. A smell I have never wanted to endure, for an endurance it is. I don't care what people have done; this is most horrible.

A few minutes later, the police arrive, having seen the fireball go up to the sky. The three of us are sitting there, Susan wrapped up in Hans' arms, and I am just sitting, staring.

'Anyone in there?' asks the police officer.

'Yes,' I say, 'couldn't get her, couldn't get her.' The man steps forward but is beaten back by the heat as well. He shouts in his radio for the fire service.

Another officer arrives on scene and he approaches me. It's Martin Kerr and he looks at me with concern.

'Are you okay, Mr. Smythe?'

'Yes,' and then his face turns up.

'And who's that?' He asks.

'Jenny Carnegie. I came here to see what she was up to.'

Martin raises an eyebrow. 'Well, she won't be up to much anymore,' he says. There's no joke there, it's just a solemn statement.

'No,' I say, 'but then again, a lot of people will sleep safer.' Again, he looks at me inquisitively, but I don't volunteer anything. That's for later, later we can work it out. Susan looks up and sees the fire again. I reach over, pulling her to me and she sits in my lap, eyes streaming.

'Not your fault,' I say, over and over again. 'Not your fault, just an accident. Remember that it's just an accident.' I look down at the red hair and she buries her face back into my chest. I stroke it trying to sooth her, but when these things happen, they don't leave you. As evil as the woman was and now departing this earth, it still doesn't leave you.

Chapter Twenty-One

Martin Kerr stares at me across the interview room. They let me get some medical attention, which was good, because having been stabbed in the shoulder and having a couple of other flesh wounds, I was a bit sore to say the least. I also needed some time to calm down from that image of Jenny Carnegie. A woman, beautiful for her years but evil inside. Even when I saw her burn, I felt sorry for her. I think that's a good thing. People say she deserved it and she probably did. But it's not mine to dispense; that's what they told me growing up. Never mine to dispense the justice—that's God's work. Saying that, I haven't had much of a conversation with him about it recently or any time since the arm but there you go.

Martin's just completed my statement and I've told him there's a lot more I need to fill in. Martha's making her way in with Maggie. I wanted to bring Maggie in to see Susan, who's still a mess, but also to try and bring in what she's got, evidence-wise. The police have raided Jenny Carnegie's place, looking for evidence there as well, and hopefully along with whatever Martha can give them and what we've seen, things should get shut down really quick.

I also tell him about Anna and some of the others, who should now be able to cooperate. In some ways, this might be easier with Jenny Carnegie passed on. With the head gone—and I have little doubt she was the head—people can speak more freely.

I still feel cold, numb, despite the tea I've poured into me. It's pretty rubbish tea when it's hot, but at this hour of the morning at least it's something. Martin says he's going to have to talk again to me, and I nod, telling him I'm at his full disposal. He says it's quite a tale, especially when he asked me why I didn't call him in sooner. Having done so, he then disappears off to come back half an hour later, saying that my call was intercepted by Gillespie and that's why he came after me.

Gillespie's in a cell at the moment, he advises me, telling me he's got trouble with the rest of the troops, keeping their hands off Gillespie. He thinks it's one bad egg and that we both hope that that's all it is. I mean, being on the force, I know the dedication of the people and I know the betrayal they'll feel but that's their problem. I left that world a long time ago.

When I step out of the interview room to the front of the station, Maggie runs over to me. She throws her arms around me, and this is a nice change. These last six months, being able to come home and see somebody happy to see me instead of going back to an empty boat is all the difference in the world. Susan's getting more attention, a doctor assessing her thoroughly for shock. She'll have to make a statement as well, and I doubt we'll be clear before lunchtime.

On the bright side, the woman they kidnapped is fine. She's in the local hospital having ingested some water when she hit the river, but that's more as a precaution. They're expecting her to walk out tomorrow. I realize I still don't even know her name. But it's something I can rack up against the death of

Jenny Carnegie. One lived while the other didn't, and I'm glad which one did.

That afternoon, I spend back at Craigantlet. Susan sleeps outside in the main cabin, Martha watching over her. Hans crashes in the digs at the far end of the boat. And I get back into my proper bunk, with Maggie beside me. I can feel her hand tracing over the wounds and the scars.

'She was some operator,' says Maggie. 'Every time she was in here, the way she was flashing things at you, using her legs, the eyes, everything, every word going for you. I could have killed her then.'

'But you didn't, and a lot of people are safe now. I'm sorry, sorry to put you through that but I know you trust me.'

There's a smack on my backside. 'Of course, I trust you, but I didn't trust her,' she says. 'And you men are stupid and weak.'

My hand flies backwards and starts tickling her belly. 'Enough of that.'

'Well, it's true,' she says. 'Look at her husband. He actually calls you in to investigate her, when he's got no idea what she's even up to. I mean why?'

'According to Martin Kerr, it's because she allowed him back in the bed again. Seems she had a fun time while this was all going on, which makes her a very busy woman.'

'She only had one man she was after, really, didn't she? The guy they caught with all the loot.'

'Yes, and I'm glad they caught him because that was the whole thing. How does he explain away that many millions? You can't, but until it got deposited somewhere, it was invisible. But there's also been lives ruined and we've got two dead. The police said they were going to investigate the hoodlums that did it, or at least they think did it. Who knows if they'll be able to pin it on them but they'll certainly give it a good go. A lot of it depends if Gillespie sings. Although with all that's going on and now McAvoy's talking, I think they might do all right, put them away for some time.'

'It's going to leave an awkward community here though, those who gave in and those who didn't,' Maggie points out. I turn over, place a kiss on her forehead and then on her lips.

'And that's none of our business. I take the job, I take the money, I go home, and what goes on after that is none of my business. Besides, we've got enough to do in looking after Susan after what she saw.

I see Maggie's worried face and she nods before her hands runs across my chest. 'And I need to look after you.'

'Well, the first thing I need is some decent sleep.'

Her leg snakes around mine, and Maggie hauls herself on top of me. 'I said I was going to look after you, not just put you to bed!'

It's about eight o'clock at night when we're all up and moving again. We take the tender over and find a restaurant to eat in. There's quite a solemn mood amongst us, and yet I know that we won. When it comes to investigative work, this is a win—we uncovered the mess. Unfortunately, we weren't quick enough to stop the two deaths. And it would have been better to see Jenny pay for her crimes in a jail and not with her life. But I'm happy. This could have gone a lot worse.

As I'm sitting over my steak and chips, with a greasy fried egg on top, a woman comes into the restaurant. I recognize her as Anna and pull up a chair for her, but she waves her hands saying no.

'Just to say thanks, Mr. Smythe. I can build again, I can get on.' It's hard looking up at that face. The taut skin with young cheekbones and the eyes that are so haunted for such a young person, but which now seem to have hope in them as well.

'All the best with it,' I tell her. 'I hope your life gets better from here on in.' She steps forward and takes my hand before turning away. I wonder how much better she thinks it feels. Maybe she saw everybody together and realized what she missed. Maybe it was Maggie's arm around my shoulder as I spoke to her. Maggie wasn't to know but maybe that wasn't the best idea.

The following day, I drive out in the car with Maggie. Martha stays on board the boat, working a few more angles to try and pass more information to the police. I have to drop into the station in the afternoon, so I take the morning off with Maggie and we head out to the Fairy Pools. I like to go back to places, especially somewhere traumatic, to see if I can see the beauty again. There's just tape at the car park, so we have to park elsewhere. The scene at the Fairy Pools is cordoned off, forensic teams still working, so we walked back down to the first one where I saw Jenny dance that first time.

'And tourists actually came to watch this?' says Maggie, sounding deeply unimpressed.

'Oh, yeah, and I get it. I mean, when you saw her, when she was out dancing there, she was teasing, she was putting it out for men to look and stare. But she was an operator because behind it, she was passing on how to extort, how to hurt. I never get how such beauty and how such evil sit together in a person.' Turning to Maggie I say, 'At least I don't have that in you.'

'There are dark enough things in here. Don't search too deep.' That makes me wonder what on earth she's talking about but that will have to be for another day.

After talking to the police that evening and finishing up

sometime around eleven o'clock, I get back to the boat. The following day, we drop Martha ashore, and together with Hans, they head off back to their respective homes. Susan tries to fob us off, telling us to go and finish off our holiday, but I'm not happy with how she is. In the middle of the night on the boat, she was screaming. It'll just take time and she'll get there, but she blames herself for what's happened.

The following day, we take the boat and we sail south, taking ourselves under the Skye bridge and down the narrow channels until we reach Mallaig. From there, we head across to Rhum. I moor up just off the island and I tell Maggie we're here for a week, to which she smiles. Susan takes the tender ashore, four days walking on the island, but back on board at night. I take the chance to lie out on deck, enjoying the sun with Maggie.

'If you could get that many millions,' says Maggie, 'where would you run with me? Where would we meet?'

'I don't know. I'm quite at home here but maybe over the other side, maybe Ballycastle. Have a separate place there as well.'

'Do you know where they were running, Jenny and Simon Hilden?'

'They never said but I reckon it was South America. They were going to sail, getting themselves out of the way, probably right across the Atlantic, maybe. Or maybe they intended to go round Europe, south towards the top end of Africa, hang out there for a bit before making their way across.

'But where would you go, Paddy?'

'I told you, I'm quite happy here and so was Simon Hilden. When I was inside their house overhearing them, they were standing on a balcony and it was like it was his balcony and the place he wanted this woman. It's funny, I don't think I could be that attached to a place like that.'

'No,' says Maggie, 'you just want me with your mistress.'

I open my eyes, looking shocked. 'What the heck do you mean?'

'This is your mistress,' and she taps the hull of the boat. 'But it's okay, you can share her with me any day. This is one balcony I'm happy to be on.'

And with that, I close my eyes. There's nothing like the Scottish coast and there's nothing like lying on a deck like this with your woman by your side. But you need the light breeze that comes from the sea and that slightly cool air that takes the edge off the sun. If it was like this for all of summer in Scotland, you can forget any of those other places. People would flock here.

'Anyway,' I say, 'with that many millions I'd fly.'

'Shush,' says Maggie, 'don't upset her feelings, never scorn your mistress.' She gives me a dig in the arm, and I roll over wrapping her up in my arm.

Yeah, she's right . . . this is my mistress.

About the Author

GR Jordan is a self-published author who finally decided at forty that in order to have an enjoyable lifestyle, his creative beast within would have to be unleashed. His books mirror that conflict in life where acts of decency contend with self-promotion, goodness stares in horror at evil, and kindness blindsides us when we at our worst. Corrupting our world with his parade of wondrous and horrific characters, he highlights everyday tensions with fresh eyes whilst taking his methodical, intelligent mainstays on a roller-coaster ride of dilemmas, all the while suffering the banter of their provocative sidekicks.

A graduate of Loughborough University where he masqueraded as a chemical engineer but ultimately played American football, Gary had worked at changing the shape of cereal flakes and pulled a pallet truck for a living. Watching vegetables freeze at -40'C was another career highlight and he was also one of the Scottish Highlands "blind" air traffic controllers. These days he has graduated to answering a telephone to people in trouble before telephoning other people to sort it out.

Having flirted with most places in the UK, he is now based in the Isle of Lewis in Scotland where his free time is spent between raising a young family with his wife, writing, figuring out how to work a loom and caring for a small flock of chickens. Luckily, his writing is influenced by his varied work and life experience as the chickens have not been the poetical inspiration he had hoped for!

You can connect with me on:
🌐 https://grjordan.com
📘 https://facebook.com/carpetlessleprechaun

Subscribe to my newsletter:
✉ https://bit.ly/PatrickSmythe

Also by G R Jordan

G R Jordan writes across multiple genres including crime, dark and action adventure fantasy, feel good fantasy, mystery thriller and horror fantasy. Below is a selection of his work grouped together in their genres. Whilst all books are available across online stores, signed copies are available at his personal shop.

A Personal Agenda (Highlands & Islands Detective Book 7)
A terrorist kills on the Caledonian Canal. Personal trauma takes Macleod out of the investigation. Can McGrath and the team strip away the killer's masked agenda and prevent another murder?

When terrorist attacks occur in the West of Scotland, Macleod and McGrath work amidst the multitude of agencies to uncover the organisation behind it. But just as Macleod makes a startling revelation, a crisis at home removes him from the team. With the country's agencies chasing down a blind alley, can newly promoted DS McGrath pull her team together and stop one final killing?

There's no wilder face of terror than the one with a personal agenda!

The Pirate Club (Highlands & Islands Detective Book 6)
A body holding a spade in the sand amidst tales of a missing gem. An old boy's network whose members are rapidly becoming extinct. Can Macleod solve the gamester's clues before the club players are liquidated and the prize is gone forever?

In the sixth major case of Macleod and McGrath's partnership, a deadly game is being played in the search for a long-stolen jewel of fantastic wealth. Whilst former friends dispatch their new enemies, DI Macleod hunts the pieces of parchment that will lead him to the resting place of a Sultan's pride and joy, and the killers who cannot live without it. Will the pirate king emerge triumphant, or can the Inspector run their plans asunder?

When precious things seem out of reach, death may be the only compromise.

 **Highlands and Islands Detective Thriller Series**
Join stalwart DI Macleod and his burgeoning new female DC McGrath as they look into the darker side of the stunningly scenic and wilder parts of the north of Scotland. From the Black Isle to Lewis, Mull to Harris and across to the small Isles, the Uists and Barra, this mismatched pairing follow murders, thieves and vengeful victims in an effort to restore tranquillity to the remoter parts of the land.

Be part of this tale of a surprise partnership amidst the foulest deeds and darkest souls who stalk this peaceful and most beautiful of lands, and you'll never see the Highlands the same way again.

The Graves at Calgary Bay (Patrick Smythe Book 2)
A naked body found on a lonely island. A band of sailors lifting graves in the dead of night. Can Paddy discover the secret that led a sheltered young man to a most gruesome death?

In his second full novel, former one-armed policeman Patrick Smythe takes to the Isle of Mull at the request of a distraught mother, looking for the truth of why her only son was found dead on the small island of Gometra. Along with his new feisty assistant, Susan Calderwood, Paddy uncovers the true story of a brutal death and incurs the wrath of a local smugglers, sailors and a well-known photographer. But when things turn nasty, can Paddy plot a way out and see that justice is done?

"The Graves at Calgary Bay" is the second full Patrick Smythe novel and continues the tale of the Ulster sleuth as his work takes him to the Isle of Mull, and the lonely island of Gometra. If you love underdogs and smart, dogged hounds of the truth, then you will love the adventures of Paddy and his red-haired teenage understudy.

Those who mess with the dead bring a reckoning onto themselves!

Lightning Source UK Ltd.
Milton Keynes UK
UKHW010626120521
383578UK00001B/65

9 781912 153800